THE TAMING OF
XANDER STERNE

THE TAMING OF XANDER STERNE

BY

CAROLE MORTIMER

First published in Great Britain 2015
by Mills & Boon, an imprint of Harlequin (UK) Limited,
Large Print edition 2015
Eton House, 18-24 Paradise Road,
Richmond, Surrey, TW9 1SR

© 2015 Carole Mortimer

ISBN: 978-0-263-25648-2

Harlequin (UK) Limited's policy is to use papers that are natural, renewable and recyclable products and made from wood grown in sustainable forests. The logging and manufacturing processes conform to the legal environmental regulations of the country of origin.

Printed and bound in Great Britain
by CPI Antony Rowe, Chippenham, Wiltshire

Our son Peter.
We are so proud of you!

CHAPTER ONE

'I APPRECIATE THAT you leave for your honeymoon at the end of the week, Darius, but I seriously do not need you to arrange for a live-in babysitter for me for the two weeks you're away!' Xander scowled at his twin brother across the sitting room of his London penthouse apartment.

'It's not a babysitter, just someone to help you with things you can't do yet, like getting in and out of the shower, drying off and dressing, driving.'

'We have a company driver who can do that.'

'But there's no one to help you with the rest of those things,' his brother reasoned. 'Or to cook for you.'

'For goodness' sake, Darius, it's been six weeks since I broke my leg.'

'In three places, requiring two operations to

fix. You can't even stand for longer than ten minutes at a time yet.' Darius was obviously refusing to back down on this.

Xander eyed him moodily, knowing that everything his brother said was true. 'This isn't really about what I can or can't do, is it?' He finally sighed resignedly.

Darius stilled. 'What do you mean?'

'What I *mean* is that I don't have a death wish. Yes, I drove my car when I shouldn't have, and yes, I ended up crashing into a lamppost and wrecking my car, but thankfully no one else was injured. But I didn't do it deliberately, Darius. I told you at the time I was just so angry I couldn't see straight. I was *angry*, Darius,' he repeated harshly.

'Everyone gets angry, Xander,' Darius said softly.

'My anger had been building for months.'

'I know.'

Xander blinked. 'You do?'

His twin nodded. 'You were working and playing way too hard. It was as if you were trying to avoid something or someone.'

'Lot of good that did me.' If Xander had been capable of pacing the room at that moment, then he would have.

Six weeks ago, for the first time in his life, Xander had realised that he had a temper. Not the slow-burning temper of his brother, but a fiery hot volcano that had exploded out of control, resulting in Xander wanting to beat another man to within an inch of his life.

Admittedly that man had been loudly verbally abusing the woman who had arrived with him that night at the exclusive London nightclub owned by the Sterne brothers. It was a situation reminiscent of Xander's childhood memories of the way in which his father had treated his mother.

But the desire to hit someone had shaken Xander to his core, to the point that he no longer trusted himself or his responses to situations; he had never wanted to hit anyone in his life before that night. Not even the father who had beaten him when he was a child.

Lomax Sterne had been dead for over twenty years now, after a fall down the stairs of the family's London home whilst in a drunken stupor. A death that neither his wife nor his twin sons had mourned.

Lomax Sterne had been a brute of a man and a bully, with a temper to match.

And six weeks ago Xander had terrified the life out of himself by discovering that, at the age of thirty-three, he had the same temper.

'What made you so tense in the first place, do you think?' Darius looked at him curiously.

Xander grimaced. 'I don't know. Yes, I do.' His brow cleared. 'Do you remember when we were in Toronto four months ago? Remember the chairman of Bank's Corporation? We went out to dinner with him and his wife.'

'And he talked down to her all evening,' Darius realised ruefully. 'Which was the reason we both decided we didn't want to do business with him. And the reason for your pent-up anger these past few months, I'm guessing?'

'I think it is, yes,' Xander agreed.

'You controlled it then, Xander, and you controlled it six weeks ago,' Darius insisted impatiently. 'Just let it go. It's over.'

Xander wished he could dismiss it as easily.

'I really do appreciate your moving in here the past four weeks, Darius, but I just don't think I'm up to having someone else, a stranger, living with me right now.' In truth, Xander had been looking forward to having his apartment all to himself again.

He grimaced. 'It's not that I'm ungrateful, Darius. I just didn't envisage the next two weeks of having to sit across the breakfast table every morning from the no doubt muscle-bound man, Sam Smith, who you've employed to act as both my nursemaid and watchdog while you're away.'

Darius gave a chuckle. 'It would certainly make the neighbours sit up and take notice, if they thought you were living with a man who isn't your brother.'

As one of the billionaire Sterne twins, Xander had a playboy reputation with women that had long been catalogued, and speculated about, by the media. So yes, they would no doubt have a field day with the fact that he was sharing his apartment with a man.

'Fortunately, for you, none of that is going to happen. Sam*antha* Smith is a woman,' Darius assured him dryly.

Xander sat forward. 'Sam Smith is a *woman*!'

'Nice to know that your hearing wasn't affected in the accident,' his twin taunted.

Darius had taken his own sweet time sharing that little nugget of information with him!

Xander scowled. 'You don't have to look so happy about leaving me completely at this woman's mercy for the next two weeks!'

'I'll ask her to be gentle with you,' Darius teased.

'Very funny,' Xander muttered distractedly; just the thought of having some strange woman staying here with him filled Xander with a sense of unease. 'So how is it that you know this woman?'

Darius smiled. 'She's a friend of Miranda's. She really likes her, so much so that she's asked Sam to work at the dance studio with her part-time once we're back from our honeymoon. Oh, and her little girl attends one of Miranda's dance classes.'

'Stop right there!' Xander held up a silencing hand, breathing hard in his agitation. 'You didn't mention she had a child. What does she plan to do with her daughter while she's staying here with me?'

'She's going to bring her with her, of course,' his brother dismissed as if there had never been the possibility of anything else.

'Are you completely insane?' Xander exploded as he finally struggled up onto his feet with the help of his crutches. 'Darius, I *told* you what happened to me at the nightclub six weeks ago. I told you how I lost control of myself, and now you want to bring some child to live with me? How old is Ms Smith's daughter?' He knew that Miranda's ballet school was for pupils from five to sixteen years old.

'Five, I think.'

'You plan on allowing this woman to bring a five-year-old child to stay in my apartment with me?' Xander breathed in deeply in an effort to calm himself. 'This was Andy's idea, wasn't it?' It was a statement, rather than a question. 'You told her what happened to me and—'

'You didn't say I couldn't.' Darius's eyes had narrowed in warning.

'I don't care whether or not you told Andy what happened to me that night,' Xander dismissed impatiently. 'After all, she's going to be your wife and my sister-in-law. What I *do* care about is that Ms Smith and her daughter coming to stay here is most likely Andy's way of trying to show me I'm not turning into the monster I think I am. A naive attempt on her part to make me feel better about myself.'

'Careful, Xander,' Darius warned softly.

Xander was too annoyed to heed that warning. 'Life isn't a fairy tale, Darius. Or, if it is, then I'm the monster in the story and not the prince!'

His brother gave Xander a considering look before speaking softly. 'You know, Xander, as Miranda once told me, quite succinctly as I recall,' Darius mused affectionately, 'the whole of life isn't about what you do or don't want.' He sobered. 'Putting my mind at rest apart, has it even occurred to you that Samantha Smith is a single parent? And that, as such, she might need the money I'm paying her to come here and act as your babysitter and watchdog while I'm away?'

But what if the woman did something to set off the temper he had only just discovered? What if her daughter did? Darius wouldn't find anything to laugh about then, would he? And Xander would never forgive himself if he lost his temper with either of them. That truly would make him the monster his father had been.

Darius scowled his displeasure. 'Look, as far as I'm concerned Miranda vouches for her, and the woman needs the money I'm paying her to come and live here with you while we're away. End of story.'

Xander didn't agree.

Yes, this penthouse apartment was big enough for a dozen other people to share it with him without them falling over each other; besides the six *en suite* guest bedrooms there was a full gym, a home cinema, as well as two other reception rooms, a wood-panelled study, a large formal dining room and an even bigger kitchen.

But that really wasn't the point, was it?

The *point* was that Xander didn't want to share any of that space with a woman he didn't even know, let alone her five-year-old daughter.

But what choice did he really have but to at least try? Darius had gone above and beyond brotherly love by moving into this apartment with him and taking care of him since Xander had come out of hospital four weeks ago.

Was it fair of him to now cause his brother any further worry while Darius and Miranda were away on their honeymoon?

Unfortunately, Xander already knew the answer to that question.

CHAPTER TWO

'IS MR STERNE a nice man, Mummy?' Daisy asked quietly as the two of them sat in the back of the limousine sent by Darius Sterne to collect them.

Was Xander Sterne a nice man?

Sam had only met the man once, during the interview she'd had with both Sterne brothers two days ago, while Daisy was at school.

Consequently, the question was a little difficult for Sam to answer, when Xander had left most of the talking that day to his brother. He'd only contributed to the conversation towards the end, when he had barked half a dozen questions at her about her daughter's schooling, and the amount of time Daisy would actually be spending at his apartment.

Making it clear to Sam that, while her new employer might be willing to tolerate her own presence in his home for the next two weeks, he wasn't in the least keen on having her daughter in residence as well.

An attitude that Sam wasn't particularly happy about.

But beggars couldn't be choosers.

She hadn't always been in such dire financial straits; her ex-husband, Malcolm, wasn't anywhere near as wealthy as the Sterne brothers, but he was nevertheless a successful businessman who owned a mansion in London, plus a villa in the South of France and another in the Caribbean.

Sam had been twenty to Malcolm's thirty-five, when the two of them had first met, she a lowly junior assistant and he the owner of the company. She had been instantly smitten with the suave and sophisticated, dark-haired and wealthy businessman, and apparently Malcolm had felt the same about her, so much so that within two months of meeting each other they had been married.

Sam had been starry-eyed and, to begin with, so much in love with her handsome and successful husband. Her parents had both died years ago, and she had been brought up in a series of foster homes. Her extended family was practically non-existent, with only a couple of distant maiden aunts whom she never saw.

However, Sam's pregnancy had changed her marriage irrevocably.

She and Malcolm had never discussed having children—or rather, *not* having them in Malcolm's case. It turned out that Malcolm didn't want children cluttering up his life as she discovered only when she'd excitedly told him she was two months pregnant.

At the time Sam had convinced herself that it was just a knee-jerk response to the thought of becoming a father for the first time at the age of thirty-six. Malcolm couldn't really have meant it when he suggested she terminate the pregnancy.

She had been wrong.

Their marriage had changed overnight, with Malcolm moving out of their bedroom, seemingly repulsed by the idea of Sam's body undergoing a transformation as the pregnancy continued. Even then, however, Sam had naively hoped for the best, sure that her marriage couldn't really be over after only a year, and that Malcolm would come around to the idea of fatherhood, either before or after the baby was born.

Again, she had been wrong.

Malcolm had remained in the spare bedroom, ignored her pregnancy totally, and he hadn't so much as visited her once in the clinic after Daisy was born. He had even been absent from the house when she came home carrying Daisy proudly in her arms and took her up to the nursery she had spent so many hours lovingly decorating and preparing for her beautiful baby.

Sam had struggled on for another two years trying to make her marriage work, sure that Malcolm couldn't continue to ignore his daughter's existence for ever. How could he not fall in love with his adorable baby daughter?

Except he hadn't.

At the end of that two years of struggle Sam had admitted defeat. Not only did she no longer love Malcolm, she wasn't sure she even *liked* him. How could she like a man who refused to acknowledge his own wife and daughter?

The past three years certainly hadn't been easy ones. Emotionally or financially.

Her emotions and how she dealt with them were Sam's own problem, of course. But how could a billionaire like Xander Sterne possibly understand how she had to scrape the money together, basically by going without lunches all week herself, just to be able to pay for something so trivial as Daisy's ballet lesson once a week? Something her daughter had talked of almost since she could walk and talk, and which Sam refused to disappoint her over.

Of course Malcolm, when Sam asked, had refused to contribute in the slightest to Daisy's happiness, over and above the minimum childcare payment paid into Sam's bank account once a month. An account set up in the name of Samantha Smith rather than her married name of Samantha Howard.

Her married name, along with the gifts and jewellery Malcolm had given her during their marriage, and any settlement she might have expected as Malcolm's ex-wife, either in a lump sum or monthly payment, were all things Sam had been asked to give up in exchange for Malcolm agreeing to give her full custody of her beloved daughter. A price Sam had willingly paid. And would willingly pay again, if she had to.

Xander, a man who owned and ran successful businesses globally with his twin brother, couldn't possibly understand how difficult it was for a single mother to even find a job, let alone one that necessarily fitted in with the hours Daisy spent at school. Waitressing at lunchtimes had been one of Sam's only options since Daisy started school the previous September, and even that became a nightmare when the school holidays came around. As they invariably did.

That last problem was going to be solved in two weeks' time, though, by her new job at Andy's ballet studio. In the meantime, this two weeks of looking after Mr Sterne would allow her to pay her electricity and gas bills.

Even so, it was mainly out of gratitude to

Andy that Sam was now on her way to spend two weeks in the home of a man she had only met once, and whom she wasn't in the least comfortable being around. He hadn't exactly been outright rude to her, but he hadn't exactly been polite either.

So, was her new employer a *nice* man?

Quite honestly, she had no idea.

Oh, there was no doubting that he was fiercely masculine, with his wide and muscled shoulders, narrow waist and hips, and long legs. His hair was a tousled and overlong gold, and his eyes were a dark and piercing brown in his tanned and chiselled face; nose long and straight between sharply etched cheekbones, his mouth full and sensual, with the top lip fuller than the bottom above a square and determined jaw. As an indication of a sensual nature?

Well, probably not the latter for the past six weeks, since his car accident had resulted in a badly broken leg and basically kept him as being almost a recluse in his own apartment.

Although that obviously wouldn't have prevented women from visiting him at home!

It was something Sam hadn't thought of until now, but the bedroom exploits of billionaire Xander Sterne had been making the headlines in the newspapers and glossy magazines for more years than Sam cared to contemplate.

And the women photographed draped on his arm, at film festivals and other celebrity events, were always beautiful, always single, and always long-legged and oozing sex appeal.

'Mummy?' Daisy's curious tone reminded Sam that she hadn't yet answered her daughter.

She turned to give her daughter a beaming smile. 'Mr Sterne is a very nice man, darling.' She avoided so much as glancing in the direction of the chauffeur sitting in the front of the car—just in case she should happen to catch his sceptical gaze in the rear-view mirror as confirmation of her misgivings.

Because nice was hardly a word anyone would use to describe Xander. Dynamic. Arrogant. Lethally attractive. But nice? Not so much.

'Will he like me, do you think?' Daisy added anxiously.

It was her daughter's anxiety that made Sam's mouth tighten. It was a legacy of all these years of Malcolm's total lack of interest in his young child and an uncertainty that had resulted in Daisy being nervous around all men.

'Of course he'll like you, poppet.' Sam would rip the arrogant Xander Sterne to shreds if he did or said anything to hurt her already vulnerable daughter. 'Now, did you remember to pack teddy in your bag?' She deliberately changed the subject; there was really no reason to worry Daisy when she, herself, was already nervous enough for the both of them.

Xander didn't exactly pace the hallways of his apartment so much as clomp inelegantly up and down them on his crutches, as he waited impatiently for the arrival of Samantha Smith and her young daughter.

Xander had to admit to being a little surprised by Sam's appearance when she'd arrived at his apartment on Wednesday morning, so much so that he hadn't been able to so much as speak for most of the interview, but had instead left Darius to do all the talking.

For one thing, she must have been a child bride, because she didn't look as if she could be any older than her early twenties, certainly not old enough to be the mother of a five-year-old.

For another, she was very tiny, maybe a dot over five feet tall, and almost as slender as his future sister-in-law. Although the weary shadows about her arresting amethyst-coloured eyes, and the hollows in her pale cheeks, looked as if she owed her slenderness more to a lack of eating rather than the hours of dance practice that Miranda enjoyed.

Those unusual amethyst-coloured eyes weren't the only arresting thing about Ms Smith's face; she also had high cheekbones, with a smattering of freckles over those hollow cheeks and bridge of her pert little nose, and a full and sensual mouth. Her hair, brushed back from her face and secured at her crown but still long enough to fall silkily to midway down her back, was a deep and vivid red colour. And surely indicative of a fiery nature?

If it was, then Xander had seen little of that fire during that half-hour interview two days ago. Instead, the woman had spoken quietly in answer to first Darius's questions, and then his own, her long dark lashes lowered as she barely glanced at him long enough for him to enjoy those unusual amethyst eyes.

Maybe she was shy, or maybe she just didn't approve of or like playboy billionaires, but was willing to put up with him for the sake of the large amount of money Darius was paying her? His brother had preferred to attribute her quietness to nervousness at being the focus of the attention of both Sterne brothers.

Which was highly possible, Xander accepted ruefully; Darius on his own or Xander on his own could be intimidating enough, but put the two of them together…

Whatever the reason for her introspection on Wednesday, Xander was only willing to put up with her mouse-like company long enough for

Darius and Miranda to enjoy their wedding and honeymoon, and not a moment longer.

So where the hell was she? Paul had left to collect the woman and her daughter over an hour ago. It was not an auspicious start to her employment here, if she hadn't even been ready to leave at the agreed time.

Xander needed to talk to Ms Smith as soon as she arrived, and make it very clear from the onset what he would or would not tolerate from her young daughter. He already had a mental list of rules prepared.

No running up and down the hallways of his apartment.

No shouting or screaming.

No loud television programmes, especially in the mornings.

No going anywhere near his bedroom suite.

And absolutely no touching any of his artwork or personal things.

In fact, Xander would prefer it if he wasn't even made aware of the child's presence in his apartment. Was that even possible with a five-year-old?

It would have to be. Ms Smith and her daughter weren't his guests but employees, and Xander expected her, and her daughter, to behave accordingly.

'Oh, look, Mummy, have you ever seen such a big television?'

Xander barely had a chance to register the presence of the woman and her young daughter, after the doors opened to his private lift, before a small red-haired whirlwind rushed past him down the hallway in the direction of the open door to the home cinema. She clipped his elbow as she passed, which knocked him off balance. Enough so that Xander felt himself falling.

Sam's stricken gaze followed her daughter's headlong flight down the carpeted hallway with all the horrified fascination of someone watching an unstoppable train wreck.

She closed her eyes with a wince as Daisy rushed past an open-mouthed Xander Sterne, opening them again just in time to see him swaying unsteadily on his feet.

Yep, definitely a train wreck!

Sam quickly dropped her shoulder bag onto

the floor in order to run down the hallway, reaching Xander Sterne's side just in time to put a supportive shoulder underneath his arm to prevent him from toppling over completely.

Or, at least, that was the plan.

Unfortunately, Xander weighed probably twice as much as she did. So that when he overbalanced completely he took Sam down with him, both of them ending up on the floor, the fall slightly cushioned by the thick carpet but still eliciting a grunt from Xander Sterne as he landed on his back, Sam sprawled inelegantly across him, her denim-clad legs entangled with his much longer ones.

This wasn't just a train wreck, it was a disaster!

'Well, that's rule number one already null and void!' he muttered through gritted teeth.

'Sorry?' Sam raised her head to look down at him.

'Why are you and Mr Sterne lying on the floor, Mummy?' a bewildered Daisy enquired curiously as she wandered back down the hallway to look down at them.

'Will you tell her or shall I?' Xander Sterne's chest—his very muscled chest beneath another fitted black T-shirt—moved beneath Sam's breasts as he bit the words out.

Sam felt the colour warming her cheeks as she realised her eyes were just inches away from the censorious brown ones now glaring up at her, and that her boss's chiselled features were twisted in displeasure.

Or perhaps it was pain he was exhibiting rather than censure?

Daisy had just succeeded in knocking this man over when he was still recovering from a broken leg, the very reason that she and Daisy were in his apartment in the first place.

'I'm so sorry,' Sam mumbled as she moved carefully, to avoid hurting Xander further, lifting herself up and away from him before standing up. She wondered whether she ought to answer her daughter first or help him back up onto his feet.

She decided to do both as she noted that his face had paled in the last few minutes.

'We fell over, darling,' she answered Daisy

distractedly as she went back down onto her knees beside Xander. 'Should I call your doctor before you attempt to get up, do you think?' she prompted worriedly as he began to roll onto his right side—the side with the leg that wasn't broken—with the obvious intention of attempting to get back up onto his feet.

Xander turned to give her a cold stare, knowing it was his dignity that was injured more than his leg. Four weeks of hobbling around on crutches hadn't exactly been good for his ego, and now he had to deal with the fact that he had been knocked off his feet by a child.

Although it hadn't been all bad, Xander acknowledged grudgingly as he reached for his crutches to help him to his feet; Ms Smith might be a tiny little thing, and her build a bit too much on the slender side for his normal taste, but what little of her there was was completely feminine. A fact his body had definitely responded to as she lay sprawled on top of him. Her body had felt incredibly soft, and she'd smelt of flowers.

It was good to know, after six weeks without sex, that at least that part of him was still in working order, even if the rest of him was still shot to hell.

Even if it was an entirely inappropriate response to the woman being paid to share his apartment for the next two weeks.

'I don't need a doctor to know that the only part of me that's bruised is my ego!' Xander answered her more harshly than he had intended. Slightly regretting that harshness as she appeared to recoil and withdraw into herself.

What had she expected? That he was just going to laugh it off as childish exuberance?

Damn it, she and her daughter had only just arrived; he hadn't even had chance as yet for the talk about rules regarding her daughter's behaviour.

'Ah, just in the nick of time,' Xander muttered as the lift doors opened a second time and Paul stepped out carrying several bags, obviously the mother and daughter's luggage. 'Paul can help me get up, if you would like to take your daughter with you into the kitchen and make a pot of tea,' he bit out.

Sam knew it was an order rather than a request, and a means of getting she and Daisy out of the way.

And who could blame the man? He had already suffered the indignity of being knocked off his feet; he didn't need the further embarrassment of having to be helped back up in front of an audience.

Xander Sterne didn't give the impression he was a man who liked to show any sort of weakness. Ever. Which didn't bode well for the next two weeks, Sam acknowledged with a wince, when she was supposed to be helping him, as well as cooking for him.

She gave Paul a grateful smile before leaving him to help Xander back onto his feet, while she and Daisy went down the hallway in search of what turned out to be a beautiful red and black high-gloss kitchen, its numerous and expensive appliances all in gleaming chrome.

The sort of kitchen that she would have loved to explore further, if she weren't feeling quite so much trepidation about whether or not she and Daisy would be here long enough for her to see any more of this apartment than the kitchen. And the inside of the lift again, as they left!

She lifted Daisy up onto one of the bar stools before finding a carton of orange juice in the huge American-style fridge, and pouring some into a glass for her.

'I thought we had a rule about running in the house?' she chided Daisy gently as she moved to put the kettle on before looking for the tea, aware of the murmur of male voices out in the hallway as she did so.

'Sorry, Mummy.' Her daughter gave a guilty grimace. 'I just saw the huge television and I wanted to— Sorry,' she muttered again contritely.

Sam's expression immediately softened. 'I think you owe Mr Sterne an apology for running in his home, don't you?'

'Yes, Mummy. Do you think he'll let us stay now?' Daisy added anxiously.

It didn't help that Sam was wondering the same thing.

She raised her brows. 'Do you want to stay?'

'Oh, yes,' Daisy enthused.

Sam had no doubts that the huge TV was the reason for her daughter's enthusiasm. It certainly couldn't be because Daisy liked Xander Sterne, when all he had done so far was growl at them.

Xander had just been about to enter the kitchen, with the intention of giving the woman a blistering piece of his mind before then ordering her to leave, when he overheard the conversation between mother and daughter.

At which point his chest gave a tight and unexpected squeeze at how subdued the previously exuberant Daisy now sounded.

Because he had reacted like a bad-tempered idiot. To a five-year-old.

Damn it, he was *not* turning into his father. He was not!

It wasn't as if the little red-haired tornado had *meant* to knock him off his feet. It had been a complete accident that she had managed to clip his elbow as she passed.

But why was he making excuses for her, when he had just been presented with the perfect opportunity—the perfect excuse—to dismiss

Ms Smith? Before she'd even had chance to unpack the few belongings in the bags he had instructed Paul to leave out in the hallway before he left.

And what happened if Xander did dismiss her? He did still need her help and he would mess up Darius and Miranda's honeymoon plans if he dismissed her now.

The fact that Sam might be counting on the money she would earn by working for him for the next two weeks was also a consideration.

Despite his reservations, even Xander wasn't selfish enough to want to be responsible for causing Ms Smith, or her daughter, unnecessary hardship.

CHAPTER THREE

SAM HAD HER back turned towards Xander when he finally entered the kitchen, allowing him to enjoy the sight of that gloriously curling red hair as it flowed loosely down the narrow length of her spine, the pertness of her shapely bottom clearly outlined by her skinny jeans.

Xander veered his scowling gaze sharply up and away from all that femininity, to instead look at the little girl seated at the breakfast bar, and currently watching him with huge and anxious amethyst-coloured eyes over the top of the glass of orange juice she was drinking.

It was an anxiety Xander remembered from his own childhood.

An anxiety *he* was now responsible for causing, as his father once had for him.

Xander's knowledge and experience of children was limited, to say the least, but even he could see that the child was a beauty, with her riot of long, red curls. Her features were more rounded than her mother's, although the promise of the same beauty was definitely there. It was a cherubic face at the moment, dominated by large and serious eyes, and she had a similar endearing smattering of freckles across her cheeks and the bridge of her tiny nose.

She now struggled down from the tall bar stool to look up at him from beneath long dark lashes. 'I'm very sorry for knocking you over, Mr Sterne.'

Oh, hell, she even had an endearing lisp when she talked, caused no doubt by that noticeably missing front tooth.

'I didn't mean to,' she continued to lisp. 'It's just that I've never seen such a big television before.' Her eyes filled with unshed tears. 'But Mummy has told me re—re—'

'Repeatedly,' Samantha supplied helpfully as she placed a cup of steaming-hot tea and the sugar bowl down on the breakfast bar in front of where Xander stood.

'Re— Lots of times,' the little girl substituted endearingly, 'not to run in the house.'

'I've labelled it "the whipped puppy look",' Sam confided softly even as she ruffled her daughter's red curls affectionately.

'What?' Xander had to drag his gaze away from the contrite-looking child in order to look at her mother.

'The tears welling up in the big eyes, the trembling bottom lip; "whipped puppy" look,' the mother supplied ruefully. 'It's a look my daughter, most young children in fact, have mastered to perfection by the time they're three!'

'Oh.' How to feel foolish in one easy lesson; he was being played, and by a five-year-old, at that!

Sam gave a rueful smile as she obviously saw the confusion in his expression. 'I assure you, the contrition is perfectly genuine, and you really shouldn't feel bad about responding to "the look"; it usually works on me too.'

Xander had the distinct impression he was fast losing control of this situation. If he'd ever had control of it in the first place!

But it was well past time that he did.

Xander looked coldly down the length of his nose at the two Smith females. 'Paul left your bags out in the vestibule, which for obvious reasons you will have to carry to your rooms yourself. You have the two adjoining bedrooms on the right at the end of the hallway. My own suite of rooms is behind the doors on the left. An area that, under no circumstances, will either of you enter without permission. For any reason,' he stated decisively.

For a heartbeat or two she looked taken aback by the harshness of his tone after their earlier conversation, before she straightened her slender shoulders, seemingly unaware of how the movement thrust forward her tiny but perfectly rounded breasts.

Something Xander was completely aware of, in spite of himself.

'Of course, Mr Sterne,' she now answered him smoothly. 'Come along, Daisy, Mr Sterne wants to be alone now.' She held out her hand to her daughter, which Daisy took before turning to bestow another shy smile on Xander as they left the kitchen together.

Leaving Xander feeling like a complete boor for having spoken to the two of them so harshly.

He instantly dismissed the feeling; if Daisy Smith had that 'whipped puppy' look down to perfection, then she had almost certainly acquired it from her mother.

'Is there anything else I can get for you, Mr Sterne?'

Sam kept her expression deliberately bland as she waited beside the formal dining table where she had just served him the first course of his dinner: perfectly cooked asparagus and Béarnaise sauce.

Her long hair was secured tidily at her nape, and she was wearing the same plain white shirt and tailored black trousers she had worn to her interview earlier in the week; it was her idea of her evening 'uniform' for the next two weeks.

Sam had brought all the ingredients with her for the meals she would be serving over the weekend, knowing that she wouldn't have the time, with Darius and Andy's wedding tomorrow, to go shopping for food until Monday.

She had decided to prepare something simple for Xander's evening meal today: the asparagus, followed by steak and a fluffy stuffed potato and buttered carrots, and for dessert she had made a pineapple upside-down cake with ice cream; easy to make, but it looked and tasted good. And there was no denying that the kitchen was a dream to work in.

Sam had always liked preparing and cooking food, and it was something she knew she was good at too. Which was why she had been deeply disappointed when Malcolm had refused to allow her to cook for him, insisting that it was what he employed his chef for. The most Sam had been allowed to do in that area was to approve the menus for the week.

Unfortunately, since the separation and divorce Sam's meagre budget had been a huge deciding factor in the meals she had been able to prepare for Daisy and herself.

Happily, there would be no such limitations in Xander's household. Sam very much doubted he had ever eaten a bowl of home-made stew in the whole of his privileged life!

'What did you have in mind?' He leant back in his chair to look up at her with those dark unfathomable eyes, his only concession to changing for dinner being to replace the black T-shirt of earlier with a white one. But then, he was in his own home, and so perfectly at liberty to wear whatever he chose, whenever he chose. Or not…

It had been a couple of hours since he had dismissed Sam and Daisy from the kitchen, and Sam had made good use of that time, by unpacking their few belongings and putting them away in the empty drawers in their bedrooms. She had also put the food she had brought with her away in the fridge and kitchen cabinets, before preparing dinner.

Sam's cheeks warmed now as she heard the unmistakeable challenge in his tone. A challenge she chose to ignore. She had been married to a man whose wealth, and the power that wealth gave him, had rendered him both arrogant and selfish, to the point that Malcolm had ridden roughshod over everybody. Including Sam and her romantic dreams of their happy future together.

She had no intentions of so much as acknowledging that Xander Sterne had that bad-boy look off to perfection, in the fitted white T-shirt that stretched tautly over his wide shoulders and chest, and revealing his tanned and muscled arms. Or that she was guilty of having noticed the tautness of his bottom earlier, in those hip-and-thigh-hugging black jeans.

Enough so that it now made Sam's heart beat faster just to look at all that blatant maleness, her palms feeling slightly damp, a tingling warmth in her breasts and between her thighs.

None of which she wanted to feel for the arrogant man. 'You made a comment earlier,' she said coolly. 'Something about rule number one being null and void?'

'So I did.'

'What did you mean by it?'

'Where's Daisy?' He asked a question of his own rather than answer hers. 'It seems very quiet in the apartment this evening.' He raised questioning blond brows.

Sam's hackles were already up in regard to her daughter, but she stiffened defensively now; no matter what this man might think to the contrary, Daisy was not a noisy or a rowdy child. The opposite, in fact. Daisy was introspective rather than outgoing; no doubt a legacy of those early years of her childhood spent with a father who ignored her very existence, and had his own set of rules for ensuring he did so.

A guilt Sam still lived with on a daily basis.

For having ever held out even the fragile hope her marriage would one day return to their first year together, when she and Malcolm had seemed so happy together. For hoping, praying, that Malcolm would one day come to love his beautiful daughter.

She had wasted almost three years hoping and praying for those things, not just of her own life but of Daisy's too, and on a man Sam had belatedly realised she wasn't sure she had ever really known, let alone loved. A rich and arrogant man who had seen his much younger wife only as an asset, to be paraded on his arm, and to fill his bed at night. A man who was too selfish, too self-absorbed, to love the beautiful daughter they had made together.

Xander Sterne was even richer and more powerful than Malcolm could ever hope to be, and Sam didn't even want to acknowledge that he was also far more disturbingly attractive too. That he possessed a sensual magnetism she responded to, however unwillingly.

Her days of allowing herself to be attracted to rich and powerful men were long gone!

Having been forced to live by a set of rules once, Sam wasn't sure she could now adhere to another set, laid down by Xander Sterne for the time she and Daisy would be staying with him in his apartment.

'Samantha?'

She blinked before focusing on the man now studying her with piercing eyes beneath long lashes.

'Sam,' she invited automatically.

'I prefer Samantha,' he dismissed arrogantly—as if that settled the matter.

Which in Xander Sterne's self-assured eyes, it probably did. And really, what did it matter whether this man called her Sam or Samantha, when in two weeks' time they would never set eyes on each other again?

'Whatever you're comfortable with,' she allowed disinterestedly. 'And to answer your question, Daisy has already been fed, bathed, and is now fast asleep in bed.'

Xander had no idea where Samantha's thoughts had been for the past few moments, but he was pretty sure they couldn't have been pleasant ones. Her eyes had taken on a haunted look, the hollows of her cheeks paler than ever against the fullness of her rose-coloured lips. 'It's only eight o'clock.'

Samantha nodded. 'Daisy always goes to bed at seven o'clock on schooldays.'

Something else Xander didn't know about children.

'Fine.' He shrugged. 'Then perhaps you and I can talk about those rules after dinner?'

Her back stiffened. 'Of course, Mr Sterne.'

'Xander.'

'I would prefer that we keep things formal between the two of us.'

'Does that mean you would really prefer that I call you Mrs Smith?'

'No, because I'm not Mrs Smith,' she answered with a humourless twist of her lips.

Xander studied her through narrowed lids. 'I seem to remember my brother telling me you're divorced?'

'I am.' She nodded tersely. 'I reverted to my maiden name after the divorce.'

He frowned. 'Is Daisy's surname Smith too?'

'Yes.' Her mouth tightened defensively.

'I don't understand.'

Not many people *would* understand a situation like hers. One where a father insisted upon, rather than objected to, his child's surname being changed to her mother's maiden name after the divorce. Malcolm hadn't even wanted Daisy to possess his surname.

'Your food is getting cold, Mr Sterne.' She pointed out the obvious as she once again avoided meeting his gaze. 'And I have several things that need my attention in the kitchen,' she added before he could object. 'But I'll be more than happy to have that chat after I've served your coffee.'

Xander frowned as he began to eat his cooling asparagus, his attention really on watching her as she left the dining room. He was totally aware of the defensive stiffness of her very straight spine and shoulders, and the vulnerable length of her neck as she tilted her head back just as defensively.

Obviously he had said something to upset her—something *else* to upset her!

But wasn't it a little unusual to also change a child's surname after a divorce?

Not that he was acquainted with divorce on a personal level. His own parents had been unhappily married and probably *should* have divorced each other, but they hadn't, so that when Lomax Sterne died, Catherine and her two sons had continued to keep the surname Sterne. His mother had only changed her name to Latimer when she married Charles, Xander's stepfather.

Xander knew he would object strongly to any

woman wanting to change *his* child's surname to her own, divorce or no divorce.

Xander gave a shake of his head; he was taking far too much of an interest in the life of his temporary employee.

'Dinner was excellent, thank you.'

Sam gave a nod of her head in acceptance of the praise as she placed the tray of coffee things down on the dining table.

'Sit,' Xander invited tersely as she began to clear the dessert bowl from the table.

'I'd rather stand, if you don't mind,' she said, trying not to bristle at being ordered about so impolitely.

His gaze was cool as he looked up from stirring sugar into his black coffee. 'I do mind.'

Sam gave a perplexed frown. 'I really don't think it's appropriate for maintaining our employer/employee relationship for me to join you at the dinner table.'

'I think the appropriateness or otherwise of our situation will be dispensed with the moment you have to help me prepare for bed later tonight!'

Sam instantly felt the heat of embarrassment burning in her cheeks—a blush she knew would clash horribly with the red of her hair—at this reminder that this was one of the duties she had agreed to when she took this job. A totally ridiculous embarrassment, when she had been a married woman for over three years.

Except she hadn't been married to Xander Sterne.

Xander Sterne was in a whole different category from Malcolm when it came to physical prowess. Despite the inconvenience of having had a broken leg for six weeks, which had seriously affected his mobility, he was still all lean muscle and barely leashed power.

The thought of having to help him prepare for bed later tonight, including being available in case he needed help with his shower, was enough to make Sam feel hot all over, and she had to clasp her hands tightly together behind her back so that he wouldn't see they were trembling.

'All the more reason for us to maintain the formalities between us,' she countered coolly.

Xander rarely used this formal dining room, and he hadn't enjoyed eating dinner on his own in here this evening either. So much so that he was going to instruct Samantha to serve his meals in the kitchen in future. But he couldn't help notice her discomfort at his mention of needing her help later tonight.

He wasn't exactly looking forward to the awkwardness of that experience himself, but for a few seconds Samantha had looked positively horrified at the reminder of it, before she quickly masked the emotion. An emotion that was still evident in the flush in her cheeks, and the trembling hands she had attempted to hide from him by thrusting them quickly behind her back.

Proving she wasn't quite as cool and composed as she wished to appear...

'I'm starting to get a crick in my neck from looking up at you,' he bit out impatiently.

'I'm not tall enough for you to get a crick in your neck.' She eyed him sceptically.

She had a point; even with Xander seated at the table their eyes were almost on the same level.

'Look, Samantha, I really am trying to refrain from actually ordering you to sit down,' he rasped testily.

'Why?'

'Because you obviously took exception to it a few minutes ago,' he bit out irritably.

Once again Xander watched the emotions flickering across Samantha's delicately thin face, seeing reluctance, and then irritation, as good sense obviously won out, and she pulled out the chair opposite him before lowering herself down to perch uncomfortably on its edge.

She raised her chin. 'I believe you wanted to discuss the rules for the time Daisy and I are staying here?'

That *had* been what Xander wanted to discuss with her, but now it came to it he felt like a complete and utter heel for having even mentioned the subject. It had seemed to upset Samantha earlier, and even more so now, although he had no idea why.

Admittedly, he hadn't been in the best of moods after falling over earlier but he had accepted Daisy's apology, hadn't he?

He hadn't heard so much as a peep out of the little girl for the last three hours or so. In fact, it had been so quiet he wouldn't even have known there was a child staying in his apartment.

Which was exactly what he had wished for earlier this evening, wasn't it?

His mouth thinned. 'I'm sure you'll agree there have to be some rules for the three of us living here together?'

'Which we should perhaps have discussed in more detail before I accepted the job,' she said with a grimace.

'No doubt,' he conceded impatiently.

Samantha nodded stiffly. 'The first one of those rules is no running in the hallways, I believe?'

Xander searched that pale face for either sarcasm or humour, but she gazed back at him without emotion. As if Samantha had heard all of this before, in another time and another place.

'My requests are really only a matter of common sense,' he snapped his irritation. 'For your own and Daisy's sake, as much as for my own.'

'Oh?' Samantha raised one auburn brow.

'Yes, I— Look, I'm not used to having children around me, okay?' Xander ran an exasperated hand through his hair. 'I wouldn't want to—I wouldn't want—' He wouldn't want to what? Explode in temper at that timid little girl?

Would he do that to her? Could he do that? Was that monster he had discovered inside him capable of doing something so horrible to a five-year-old girl?

Xander no longer *knew* the answer to that question; that was the problem!

His mouth firmed. 'No running in the hallways, no screaming or shouting, no loud television programmes—especially in the mornings. And, as I've already said, no entering my bedroom suite, and definitely no touching any of the artwork.'

None of which applied to her, Sam acknowledged wearily, but was all aimed specifically at her daughter.

She certainly wasn't prone to screaming and shouting, or watching loud television programmes at any time of the day or night. Nor did she have any intention of entering Xander's bedroom suite, other than those occasions when she had to help him in or out of the shower, or to dress. Nor was there any reason for her to touch any of his no doubt priceless artwork. Why would she need to? He had a cleaning service that came in twice a week to vacuum and dust and do the laundry.

All of his rules were for the benefit of her daughter.

They were very similar to the rules that Malcolm had laid down for Daisy's behaviour. Except he had gone even further once Daisy began to walk and talk, and stated that he didn't so much as want to see or hear her. At least Xander hadn't gone that far.

Sam stood up and began to walk towards the kitchen. 'That all seems perfectly clear.'

'Samantha!'

She halted abruptly but didn't turn, swallowing as she realised her throat felt clogged with emotion. With tears. For having brought her daughter into yet another household where Daisy could perhaps be seen this time, but was certainly never to be heard.

Somehow she had expected more of Xander Sterne.

Oh, she had known before she met him, from reading newspaper articles about him over the years, that he was an arrogant playboy, who played as hard as he worked. She had also been aware, when she'd met him on Wednesday, that he obviously resented needing her help while his brother was away and she had been prepared to deal with that.

But she wasn't sure she could deal with having to subdue her daughter's enthusiasm for life just to make him happy.

She was no longer interested in making any man happy. Which was the main reason Sam hadn't so much as dated once these past three years; she had vowed never to put her daughter in a situation like the one she had suffered with Malcolm for the first two years of her life.

Once again Sam reminded herself that beggars couldn't be choosers.

Perhaps not, but she didn't have to let another arrogant man dictate his terms to her, either.

She wanted this job—the money was too good for her not to want it—but there was only so much she was willing to put up with in order to keep it.

Sam turned sharply on her heel, an angry flush in her cheeks as she glared across the dining room at Xander Sterne. 'I heard what you said, Mr Sterne, and I'll do my best to see that you aren't unnecessarily inconvenienced by having Daisy here. But I won't go any further than that.' She met his gaze challengingly now. 'If you aren't happy with that, then perhaps you should say so now and Daisy and I can leave tomorrow morning so that other arrangements can be made for you?'

Samantha was magnificent when she was angry. Her red hair, even though it was confined in a band at her crown, seemed to bristle and shimmer with electricity, her eyes glowed a deep amethyst, and her cheeks were flushed.

Her nipples were also tight against the fitted white shirt she was wearing.

Not that Xander was stupid enough to say any of that out loud; in his experience, and contrary to what a lot of other men believed, most women did not appreciate being told they looked magnificent when they were angry. Not surprising, when it sounded so damned patronising.

'I'm fine with the present arrangement,' he rasped dismissively, knowing his love for Darius and Andy gave him no real choice in the matter. But that didn't mean he had to like it!

Samantha blinked, her expression uncertain now. 'You are?'

'Do you consider any of my requests to be unreasonable? And they are requests, Samantha, not rules. If there is a problem, then tell me so now, so that we can discuss it.'

'I— Well— No.' She looked disconcerted. 'But obviously Daisy is a child and—'

'It will be fine,' Xander bit out impatiently

as he stood up from the table, his hand resting on the back of his chair for balance. 'Have you been divorced long?' he asked, the sharp shift in conversation catching Samantha off guard.

'Three years,' Samantha answered woodenly, her gaze no longer meeting his.

'Bad divorce?'

'Is there such a thing as a good one?'

'Probably not.' Nevertheless, Xander couldn't help but feel dissatisfied with her answer. Again.

All of the answers Samantha had given him so far, concerning her marriage and divorce, had been ambiguous, to say the least.

Darius had been right when he accused Xander of having become too self-centred in the weeks since his accident, deliberately so, after what had preceded that accident.

No matter how much Xander might wish it were otherwise, the arrival of Samantha and Daisy in his apartment now seemed to have made it impossible for him to continue to maintain that aloofness.

In fact, since their arrival earlier this evening

Xander had felt a burning and increasing curiosity to learn all and everything there was to know about the woman who was to share his apartment for the next two weeks.

As much, it seemed, as Samantha was determined not to tell him.

Just what was she hiding?

'Have you and Miranda known each other long?' Xander decided to try a different approach to find out what he really wanted to know.

Samantha frowned slightly before answering him cautiously.

'Andy and I met six months ago, when Daisy started taking ballet lessons.'

He nodded. 'When I talked to Andy earlier in the week she spoke very highly of you.' He wasn't about to admit how protective his almost sister-in-law had been about Samantha and her young daughter. To the point where Andy had warned him to keep his hands to himself where her friend was concerned!

Xander had found the warning amusing at the time; after all, he couldn't even stand on his own two feet without the assistance of his crutches at the moment, so he was hardly likely to be making a move on the woman.

After spending just a few hours in Samantha's company, however, he found himself definitely regretting that lack of mobility.

'That's very kind of her.' Samantha smiled. 'Andy's very easy to get along with.'

Xander nodded. 'I bet Daisy is good at ballet too?'

Her smile became openly affectionate. 'She loves it.'

'And does Daisy spend much time with her father?'

Sam drew in a sharp breath as she realised that Xander had been lulling her into a false sense of security these past few minutes, and that he had now decided to pounce. No wonder he and his brother were so successful in business; most people would know, from a single meeting, to be cautious where the brooding Darius was concerned, but they would feel less of a need with the supposedly easy-going Xander.

But perhaps she was being unfair, and Xander hadn't had this hard edge to him before his car accident six weeks ago?

No, he'd still have had the edge, Sam decided ruefully, he just chose to hide it behind that easy-going charm. A charm he was making no effort to maintain in front of her. And why should he? She was here to work, not be charmed into his bed as so many other women had been.

Her eyes narrowed. 'Daisy will be spending all of her time here with me for the next two weeks when she isn't at school.'

'That didn't exactly answer my question.'

Sam maintained that steady eye contact. 'I thought it did.'

His mouth firmed. 'Is your husband away?'

'Ex-husband,' Sam corrected. 'And I have no idea whether he's away or not. Now if you will excuse me?' she added briskly as she gathered up the used dessert bowl. 'I still have to tidy up in the kitchen.'

'It can wait.'

'I'm tired, Mr Sterne, and would like to relax for a while before bedtime,' she stated firmly.

Xander only just managed to bite back his frustration with the way Samantha continued to avoid or refused to answer any of his questions about her marriage or her ex-husband. Deepening the mystery she was fast becoming to him.

Because there was something very intriguing about the way she clammed up every time Xander so much as mentioned her ex. And the fact that she had no idea whether or not he was even in the country, let alone when he would be seeing his daughter again, was decidedly odd.

When *did* the man see his daughter?

More importantly, what had the other man done to Samantha to cause those shadows in her eyes every time the subject of him was so much as mentioned?

CHAPTER FOUR

'ARE YOU GOING to stand in the doorway all night or do you actually intend to come into the room, where you might actually be of some use in helping me?' Xander Sterne rasped impatiently from where he sat on the side of the huge four-poster bed that dominated his bedroom.

Sam had taken one look at Xander and frozen where she stood, her heart pounding in her chest and her pulse racing.

But she wasn't drooling.

At least, she hoped she wasn't.

Surely any woman could be forgiven for finding herself momentarily unable to move or speak after being confronted with an almost naked Xander Sterne?

Almost, because he had a small towel secured

about his waist that only just covered his—well, it just about covered his modesty.

Not that he had any reason to feel in the least modest from where Sam was standing.

And looking.

She was captivated by the sight of his completely bare, tanned chest and wide, muscled shoulders. His chest was covered in a fine dusting of golden hair, a six-pack rippling at his abdomen.

Sam's fascinated gaze shifted lower as he stood up, drawn to the long lean length of his bare and muscled legs, the temporary cast he wore in the day having been removed in preparation for his shower, and revealing the reddened scars from his operations six weeks ago.

Even his feet were attractive: long and elegant. Very long and elegant, Sam acknowledged slightly breathlessly, her gaze moving higher as she recalled reading somewhere that the length and size of a man's foot was in direct proportion to his—

'Samantha!'

She gave a guilty start as she reluctantly

dragged her gaze away from the concealing towel to look up into Xander Sterne's handsome but obviously impatiently irritated face.

'Sorry.' She moved briskly into the bedroom and approached where he now stood beside the bed, her cheeks feeling warm with embarrassment as she realised she was behaving like a starstruck teenager.

Come to think of it, Xander wouldn't look out of place in any action movie, his perfect form blazoned across the big screen.

'Samantha…!' Xander now sounded exasperated rather than just annoyed by her obvious distraction.

'I can't continue standing unaided for too much longer, Samantha,' he reminded harshly.

No, of course he couldn't.

Just because Xander was the most glorious male specimen she had ever seen, on or off the big screen, that was no reason to keep ogling him as if he had the starring role in her favourite sexual fantasy.

'I'll go and turn on the shower,' Sam told him as she put an instant stop to *those* thoughts, her gaze shifting sharply away from continuing to look at all that breathtaking manhood as she walked towards the bathroom, needing a few minutes alone in order to pull herself together.

Which didn't mean her thoughts didn't continue to churn as she distractedly opened the smoked-glass door to the shower that ran the length of one wall of the bathroom, her gaze becoming unfocused as she drifted off into thought again after she had turned on the water and stood waiting for the temperature to adjust.

Responding so viscerally to her boss's nakedness was something Sam hadn't expected! Especially with a man who was even more wealthy and powerful than her ex-husband. She hadn't so much as *looked* at another man since leaving Malcolm, let alone reacted so physically to one! Her breasts felt uncomfortably tingly, her nipples highly sensitive.

Sexual arousal.

For Xander Sterne, of all people.

And because she had never in her life been this close to such a gorgeous—and very naked— man before tonight; Malcolm had *never* looked so blatantly, predatorily male, not even when the two of them had first met. Malcolm never *could* have the physique and looks of Xander, not in a million years of working out at the gym three times a week.

No doubt Xander had been using his gym here in the apartment these past few weeks in order to maintain that upper-body physique.

As for his lower body…

No doubt he usually maintained that by carousing all evening and having sex all night! Although he certainly wouldn't have been able to indulge in the sex part of that since his accident.

At least, Sam presumed that he hadn't?

Which reminded her that she had one rule of her own, regarding his own behaviour, while she and Daisy were staying here, that she still needed to discuss with him.

'Samantha?'

Sam gave a sharp intake of breath, having been so lost in thought that she hadn't even noticed that Xander had entered the bathroom behind her.

She was so startled by his presence she spun quickly round to face him, not having realised he was standing quite so close to her, and succeeded in doing exactly as Daisy had earlier, accidentally knocking his elbow with the hand she had raised defensively.

Unfortunately, with the same result!

'Not again,' Xander had time to mutter disbelievingly as he felt himself falling sideways towards the hard marble floor of the bathroom.

Oh, yes, a concussion was definitely just what he needed to finish off this already disastrous day.

Except it didn't happen.

Somehow—and Xander had no idea how she managed it—Samantha moved quickly enough to lodge her shoulder underneath his armpit. At least arresting his fall, even if they did both still stagger as his weight once again proved too much for her, before they were able to drop down onto the marble ledge running along the length of the bathroom wall opposite the shower.

'You know,' Xander snapped as he righted

himself on the marble seat, 'I'm not sure if you and Daisy aren't determined to break my other leg—or worse!'

It certainly must look as if they were, Sam acknowledged with a guilty wince, shifting uncomfortably as she realised she was still tucked cosily beneath Xander's arm. Her hand, having fallen onto the firmness of his abdomen, was lying dangerously close to the top of the towel, her cheek resting against the warmth of his bared chest.

A chest that felt wonderfully solid, his skin smelling of the cologne he must have put on that morning, and a heat that spoke purely of earthy male.

It was a delicious and arousing combination.

And Sam didn't want to be aroused by this man any more than she already was. Wouldn't allow herself to be attracted to another man who believed his wealth and power gave him the right to ride roughshod over everyone else.

She jerked into a sitting position before scrambling inelegantly to her feet and moving sharply away from him. 'You startled me, creeping up on me like that!'

He eyed her exasperatedly. 'I should have guessed it was somehow going to be my fault. I'll try announcing my presence next time, shall I?'

'That might be best,' Sam replied tersely.

It was totally unfair that he looked so blatantly *male*; his overlong blond hair was tousled, and the towel, having slipped slightly during the fall, shockingly revealing more of the lean length of his thighs. Or that he so obviously felt absolutely no awkwardness at being almost naked in her presence.

But then, why should he, when he had the face and body of a Greek god? Or, more accurately, a blond Norse god.

She was absolutely not going there!

Not just because an attraction to him would be a mistake on her part, but she had Daisy to think of too.

Sam turned away abruptly. 'You should get in the shower now; it's starting to steam up in there.' She opened the glass door in readiness.

'I believe that's what I was trying to do earlier,' he bit out.

Sam kept her gaze averted as she heard Xander limping across to where she stood, her cheeks feeling warm as she heard the rustle of the towel before he held it out for her to take.

'Oh, for—!' Xander sighed his impatience as he saw that Samantha couldn't even look at him directly. 'Go and wait in the bedroom if my nakedness offends you so much.'

'It doesn't!' she snapped defensively, the colour that suffused her cheeks giving lie to that claim.

'No?' Xander challenged.

'No!'

'It certainly looks to me as if it does,' he mocked.

'Then there must be something wrong with your eyesight.' Samantha grabbed the towel from him before fleeing the bathroom.

As if the hounds of hell were chasing her, Xander noted.

Because it certainly wasn't him!

He couldn't catch a snail at the moment, let

alone a fit and healthy woman determined to avoid being alone with him.

A fact his arousal seemed totally unappreciative of. 'Not going to happen tonight, I'm afraid,' he murmured to himself. 'Or for some nights to come,' he added grimly. Samantha had made it obvious she was completely unavailable.

It would have been far better for his peace of mind—and his aching body—if his carer had been that muscle-bound tattooed man.

Tattoos…

Now that was a tantalising thought. *If* Samantha did have a tattoo what would it be and *where* would it be? A flower or a butterfly, perhaps? On her shoulder? Her breast? Or maybe her lower back, at the top of the curve of that deliciously rounded bottom?

Not helping, Sterne.

And yet the image—the fantasy—lingered as he washed his hair and rinsed his aching body.

'You can turn around now. I'm perfectly decent!'

Then Xander's definition of decent must be

vastly different from her own, Sam decided as she turned to watch him as he limped awkwardly into the bedroom, another towel, only slightly larger than the previous one, secured about his naked hips. Making the decision she had made, while he was showering, not to show any reaction to his nakedness, completely null and void.

Because he was definitely perfect. But decent? Absolutely not!

He looked like a pagan god who had risen from the sea, his chest still gleaming with droplets of water from where he had obviously washed his hair in the shower, that tousled blondness appearing darker when damp, the long length of his legs obviously also still wet and dripping water onto the carpet.

'I can't bend down that far,' he drawled as he saw the direction of her gaze.

'You should have called me,' Sam said briskly.

'I didn't want to embarrass you again.'

'I wasn't—'

'Yes, you were,' he rasped harshly. 'Are.' He moved to sit on the side of the bed as he looked up at her through narrowed eyes. 'The question is why are you, when you've been married and have a daughter to prove it?'

'I told you, I'm not embarrassed.' Sam moved briskly across the room to drop down onto her knees in front of him as she began to towel dry the long length of his legs, taking care to gentle her movements on his injured leg, avoiding the several healing scars running the length of it.

'Liar,' he drawled.

Sam looked up at him sharply. 'I think you have an overinflated opinion of your own sexual prowess, Mr Sterne.'

'Not recently I don't,' he admitted.

The perfect opening... 'I should have mentioned this to you before.' Sam kept her head bent as she concentrated on drying his feet. 'I don't think—I would prefer, for the duration of our stay here, that you didn't—I realise this is an imposition,' she began again, 'but Daisy is only five, and I really don't—'

'Do you seriously think there's a danger of any woman being interested in going to bed with me the way I am at the moment?' Xander bit out harshly as he obviously guessed where her fumbling conversation was going.

What Sam *thought* was that there was a distinct possibility that women would still want to go to bed with this devastatingly handsome and sensual man, even if he were on his deathbed!

There was an innate sensuality to Xander Sterne that would no doubt still be with him when he was ninety. And the bone structure of his face was such that he would always have that chiselled handsomeness that so many women—including Sam, unfortunately—found so devastatingly attractive.

'Or that I'm even capable of making love to a woman at the moment?' he demanded.

Sam raised her brows. 'I'm sure if you were to experiment that you would find a position that was comfortable— Forget I said that,' she dismissed as she stood up quickly from drying his feet, her cheeks once again blazing with embarrassed colour.

What had she been thinking?

Too much about being in bed with Xander, that was what she had been thinking about!

'I'm intrigued, Samantha.' He now regarded her teasingly. 'Exactly what position did you have in mind?' He looked thoughtful. 'The woman on the top would probably be the most comfortable for me, I suppose.'

'Look, all I was trying to say a few minutes ago was that I know this is an imposition, but I really would prefer it if you refrained from bringing any women to your apartment for the next two weeks while Daisy and I are staying here,' she muttered exasperatedly.

He arched one blond and arrogant brow. 'Are you going to make it worth my while?'

Sam blinked. 'Sorry?'

He placed his hands on the bed behind him as he leant back on his arms, emphasising the muscles of his shoulders and arms as he looked up at her challengingly. 'What are you offering if I agree not to bring any women to the apartment while you and Daisy are staying here?'

Sam's mouth firmed at what she had been sure was a deliberate and blatant display of his masculinity, followed by what sounded like a proposition. 'I'm not offering anything in exchange for what I consider to be a reasonable and polite request.'

'That's one answer, I suppose.'

'It's the only answer you're going to get from me,' Sam assured him stiffly. 'At the risk of receiving yet another one of your less than subtle replies—do you need anything else from me tonight?'

Xander couldn't help but grin as he saw the challenge sparkling in the boldness of Samantha's gaze, and realised that he was starting to like her. Not just in a sexual way—after his physical response to her earlier, that was a given!—but he definitely approved of her spirited conversation, and her sense of humour too.

Possibly a first for him where a woman was concerned.

Over the years Xander had fallen into the habit of dating models and actresses, visually beautiful and physically desirable women. But he hadn't necessarily got to know them well enough to discover their personalities too. Mainly, because he hadn't been particularly interested in knowing them that well, as long as they were beautiful to look at and satisfied him in bed. Which really wasn't as selfishly one-sided as it sounded, because the same was true in reverse; as long as those women could be seen out and about and be photographed on the arm of the billionaire Xander Sterne, they seemed more than happy with the arrangement.

A little—a lot!—shallow of them, and him, perhaps, but the sort of wealth and power he possessed seemed to attract that type of woman.

Samantha was totally different from any of the women he had known before.

And not just because she was a divorced woman with a young daughter.

Samantha interested him in ways Xander had never even considered with any other woman. He wanted to know about *her*: her marriage, her husband, and her divorce. More importantly perhaps, what she had done and how she had lived in the years since that divorce.

And none of that had anything to do with the fact that he'd also like to take Samantha to bed.

Well, perhaps it had a little to do with it!

He certainly wouldn't say no, for instance, if

she were to offer to go to bed with him without first telling him any of those things. In any position she wanted.

Although, from the look of disgust she was shooting him now, he didn't think that was even a possibility!

'I'm good, thanks,' Xander drawled.

Sam didn't think this man was good at all. Impossible. Temperamental. Sexy. Wickedly outrageous. But he definitely wasn't good.

She straightened. 'I'll see you in the morning, then, Mr Sterne.'

'Oh, you can count on it, Samantha,' he murmured as he watched her cross the room to the door before speaking again. 'I meant to ask, do you have any tattoos?'

Sam froze halfway across the bedroom before turning slowly back to face him, her eyes wide. 'What?'

'Do you have any tattoos?' he repeated as if this were a perfectly normal conversation.

Which it certainly wasn't. 'What does that have to do with anything?'

'Ah ha, that means you do,' he murmured

with satisfaction. 'If you didn't you would have said no,' he explained at her perplexed frown.

Sam grimaced. 'Maybe I'm just too surprised by the question to have instantly denied it?'

'Still not saying no, Samantha,' he mocked, a wicked glint in his eyes as he looked her over from her head to her toes. 'Now where would you choose to have a tattoo, I wonder?'

Sam could feel the colour once again warming her cheeks under the frankness of that gaze. 'This really isn't a suitable conversation, Mr Sterne.'

'Oh, come on, Samantha, I've been stuck in hospital and this apartment for the past six weeks; surely you aren't mean enough to deny me a little entertainment?'

'The puppy-dog look doesn't look so good on you,' Sam assured him cuttingly.

'Then answer the question! Sorry.' He scowled darkly. 'I'm just—' He ran a frustrated hand through the thickness of his blond hair. 'You aren't seeing me at my best.'

'No?' Sam wasn't sure she could cope with seeing this man at his best.

'No,' he confirmed heavily. 'I was just—
What's wrong with telling me where you have
your tattoo?'

'Goodnight, Mr Sterne.' Sam turned towards
the door.

'Is it on your breast?'

Sam faltered slightly but managed to keep
on walking.

'Your shoulder?'

Why did the door suddenly seem so far away?

'Maybe your deliciously rounded bottom?'

Sam's hand shook slightly as she was finally
close enough to reach out to take hold of the
door handle.

'Or maybe it's at the top of your thigh where
only a lover would see it?'

Sam quickly pulled the handle down and
opened the door.

'Now the thought of *that* is definitely going
to keep me awake long into the night!' Xander
murmured.

'Goodnight, Mr Sterne,' she repeated firmly
before stepping out into the hallway, closing
the door behind her before leaning weakly back

against it, able to hear Xander's soft laughter echo from behind it.

The man was impossible. Worse than impossible!

And the tiny tattoo on the top slope of her left breast seemed to throb as much at the moment as it had on the day she'd had it done five years ago.

'How do you like your toast, Daisy?' Xander frowned across the kitchen at the little girl as she sat at the breakfast bar in her pyjamas, her hair a glorious tangle of red curls about her slender shoulders. 'I can do lightly golden or burnt?'

'Burnt, please,' she answered politely.

Xander had been the only one up when he'd come to the kitchen a short time ago, but that hadn't lasted for long. Daisy had appeared shyly in the doorway just a few minutes later, obviously having heard someone moving about in the kitchen, and no doubt assuming it was her mother.

Xander's first reaction was to panic. To wonder if he was up to dealing with her, or if he should just go and get Samantha.

What if Daisy spilt some juice and he lost it? What if she dropped cereal or jam on the breakfast bar, and his violent temper made another unwanted appearance?

The rage he had felt that night in the Midas nightclub had been frightening enough, but Xander knew he would never forgive himself if he verbally or physically hurt a child. As he had been hurt by his father.

After staring blankly at Daisy for several minutes Xander had forced down the panic, decided not to go and wake Samantha, but to instead test himself and offer Daisy the same breakfast he was having.

So far it was going reasonably well. He had tried to smile as he poured Daisy some juice, and his voice had remained reasonably calm when he offered to make her some toast along with his own.

He usually didn't eat breakfast at all, preferring to grab a quick cup of coffee, but he was making an exception by eating a slice of toast this morning, unsure of when he would be able to eat again.

Darius and Miranda's wedding was at one o'clock today, but the meal wasn't being served until four o'clock, to allow time for the taking of photographs after the service, and the greeting of guests at the Midas Hotel later.

As Darius's best man, Xander had his own wedding duties to take care of.

'Oh, no!' A breathless Samantha suddenly appeared in the kitchen doorway, looking almost as dishevelled as her young daughter, in a robe belted tightly about her slender waist, her red hair a wild tangle about her shoulders, her legs bare. 'I am so sorry!' She rushed into the room. 'I should have been up and getting your breakfast long before this. I must have overslept.'

'Calm down, Samantha,' Xander advised abruptly. 'Daisy and I have been managing just fine on our own, haven't we?' He placed Daisy's plate of buttered—and burnt—toast in front of her on the breakfast bar, once again congratulating himself on having got through the past ten minutes without having a single urge to lose the temper he now feared.

Although he couldn't say he was sorry that Samantha had put in an appearance.

Sam had never felt so disorientated in her life as when she woke up in a strange bed a few minutes ago, before the reality that she was currently staying in Xander Sterne's apartment came crashing down on her. A glance at the bedside clock had shown her it was already eight o'clock, way past the time Daisy usually woke her in the morning.

She had leapt out of bed, quickly pulling on and tying her robe over the vest and shorts she wore to sleep in as she hurried next door to Daisy's bedroom, only to find her daughter's bed had obviously been slept in but was now empty.

The last thing Sam had expected, after hurrying down the hallway to the kitchen, was to find her daughter sitting at the breakfast bar while Xander made and served her breakfast.

Especially when Sam was being paid—very generously—to make and serve *his* breakfast!

It didn't help that his face looked a little pale

this morning, and his limp was much more pronounced too as he hobbled about the kitchen.

Because he shouldn't be standing on his leg for any length of time yet. Because *she* was being paid to ensure that he didn't.

She had also promised him that he wouldn't even know Daisy was in his apartment, and yet here he was, the morning after their arrival, preparing her breakfast!

'I really am sorry,' Sam mumbled awkwardly as Xander poured some coffee into a mug before handing it to her.

Today he wore a fitted brown T-shirt and faded blue jeans, his feet bare on the tiled floor.

The latter no doubt because he couldn't bend down far enough to put on his own socks and shoes and she hadn't been around to do it for him.

How *could* she have been so stupid as to oversleep on her very first morning here?

Probably because she had tossed and turned in her bed for most of the night before, unable to sleep because she was so totally aware of that last conversation with Xander. Of the fact that he was lying naked in his own bed just down the hallway!

How did Sam know he was naked?

Because while he was in the shower she had searched through the drawers in his dressing table and the wardrobes for pyjamas, in readiness for when he came out of the shower. Pyjamas that simply weren't there.

A knowledge that wasn't in the least conducive to Sam being able to fall asleep once she had climbed into her own bed.

Consequently, it had been the early hours of the morning before she had managed to drift off to sleep, resulting in her oversleeping this morning.

Sam was more than a little surprised by how relaxed Daisy seemed to be in Xander's company; usually her daughter was extremely shy around men. Big men like him especially.

No doubt yet another result of Malcolm's complete indifference to his daughter. Malcolm wasn't as big as Xander, but no doubt he would appear so to a small child. A small child who knew to leave a room if Malcolm came into it.

And yet Daisy seemed perfectly happy in Xander's company.

'I have to be at Darius's apartment by ten-thirty this morning, if you could drive me over there? I'll shower there before I dress for the wedding.'

'Of course.' Sam breathed an inward sigh of relief that he seemed to have tired—for the moment!—of teasing her. And that she didn't have the ordeal of accompanying him to the shower to get through either this morning.

'Although quite how helpful I'm going to be as best man is anyone's guess,' he added bitterly.

'I'm sure that, if nothing else, Darius will welcome your moral support today.' Sam still found Darius a little intimidating, but Andy loved him very much, and surely even a man that arrogantly self-confident must be feeling a little nervous on his wedding day?

'I won't be back until late this evening,' Xander continued dismissively, 'so it's up to you what you and Daisy do with the rest of your day.'

Sam gave him a startled look. 'Er—'

'As long as you're back here in time this evening to help me shower—'

'Mr Sterne.'

'It shouldn't be a problem—'

'Xander!'

'Sorry?' He gave an irritated frown.

Sam gave an uncomfortable grimace. 'Daisy and I are invited to the wedding.'

Well, of course they were, Xander realised.

If Samantha was a good enough friend for Miranda to recommend her for this job, then she was obviously going to invite her to the wedding too…

CHAPTER FIVE

'LEAVING ALREADY?'

Sam turned from where she was helping Daisy into her coat, looking across to where Xander stood watching her, the three of them in the gold and black marble entrance hall of the fabulously exclusive London Midas Hotel, where Andy and Darius's wedding reception was still taking place. 'It's almost nine o'clock, and Daisy's tired.' She gave a rueful smile as her daughter gave a yawn.

It had been a beautiful wedding; Andy had made a beautiful bride, Darius a handsome and distinguished bridegroom. Xander's best-man speech at the reception had caused much hilarity as he'd related—as was the custom—some of Darius's more embarrassing teenage adventures. He had wisely refrained from mentioning any of his twin's more risqué adult exploits;

both the Sterne brothers had been making headlines in the newspapers for the past twelve years
regarding those!

After the delicious wedding breakfast there
had been dancing, and Andy and Darius had
made an absolutely stunning couple as they
danced that first dance alone, one so dark and
handsome the other very fair and beautiful. The
two of them had eyes only for each other as
they moved gracefully about the dance floor.

They were joined by Darius's mother and
stepfather for the second dance of the evening,
a time when Xander should have also stood
up with the chief bridesmaid, but obviously
couldn't. Instead Andy's sister Kim had danced
with her husband, Colin.

Sam had noted that Xander remained at the
top table talking to one of the other two bridesmaids.

As a friend of the bride rather than a relative,
Sam and Daisy had been seated at a table towards the back of the huge ballroom, but close
enough to be able to watch and enjoy all of
the wedding party. She had even been asked

to dance by a couple of the single male guests. Invitations she had refused, using the excuse of not wanting to leave Daisy sitting on her own.

Yes, it had been a beautiful wedding, but it had made for a long day, and at nine o'clock in the evening it really was time for her to take her sleepy daughter back to Xander's apartment.

Sam had thought she had said her goodbyes to Andy and Darius without anyone noticing, before slipping quietly out of the ballroom. Obviously she had been wrong.

She straightened. 'Darius assured me it would be no problem for you to take a taxi home later.'

'Did he?' Xander enquired mildly.

'Yes.' Sam frowned at that mildness. 'Please don't let me keep you any longer from enjoying the rest of the wedding reception. I think the bridesmaid might be missing you,' she dismissed teasingly.

In all honesty Xander was more than a little tired of the company of the bridesmaid, a young woman who seemed bound and determined on achieving the tradition of one of the bridesmaids going to bed with the best man the night of the wedding. A tradition Xander would normally have been only too happy to satisfy! But not tonight. And the excuse that his broken leg was still healing didn't seem to have deterred the woman in the slightest from succeeding in her mission!

Oh, she was attractive enough with her blonde hair, limpid blue eyes and curvaceous figure, and usually Xander wouldn't have hesitated in taking her up on the obviously blatant offer.

But instead of responding to that overt flirtation, he had found himself constantly seeking out a head of fiery red curls, both during the wedding ceremony at the church, and later during the reception.

Samantha was wearing a figure-hugging red gown that should have clashed with those red curls, but somehow only deepened the colour of her hair to a vibrant copper, adding a creamy glow to her cheeks and the tops of her breasts visible above the scooped neckline of the gown.

Something Xander had noted several other

men admiring during the wedding reception, a couple of them having approached her table and asked her to dance. Invitations she had refused with a smiling shake of her head.

Refusals that had caused Xander to smile in satisfaction.

And warning him that he was taking altogether too close an interest in the woman temporarily employed to drive and take care of him, and currently staying at his apartment.

A warning he had taken absolutely no notice of, when he saw Samantha quietly making her excuses to Miranda and Darius, before slipping from the ballroom with the obvious intention of leaving.

'You aren't,' he clipped abruptly in answer to her comment regarding the persistent bridesmaid. 'I've actually had enough for one day too, so if you wouldn't mind waiting a few minutes, while I make my own goodbyes, I'm ready to come home with you and Daisy now.'

Sam felt a little uncomfortable hearing Xander describe his apartment as home for all of them. Because they all knew, as far as she and

Daisy were concerned, it was only a very temporary accommodation.

Looking at Xander a little more closely, though, she could see that he did indeed look a little pale under his tan, and there were also dark bruises of tiredness and strain beneath his eyes. He was leaning rather heavily on the walking stick he had insisted was going to be his only walking aid at his brother's wedding.

Was it so surprising, when Xander had barely been out of his apartment for weeks, but had now spent the whole day and part of the evening socialising with his brother and Andy's wedding guests, that he was now feeling the effects of such a busy day?

'Of course.' Sam nodded. 'We'll wait out here for you.'

'Thanks.' He gave a rueful grimace as he turned awkwardly and limped back to the ballroom, leaning heavily on the walking stick as he did so.

'Xander looks tired too, Mummy,' Daisy observed softly.

'Mr Sterne, darling,' Sam corrected distract-edly, more than a little concerned for him her-self.

Daisy frowned. 'He told me this morning that I should call him Xander.'

Sam looked down at her daughter in surprise. 'He did?'

'Yes.' Daisy gave a gap-toothed smile; she looked adorable in the amethyst-coloured knee-length party gown that had been bought espe-cially for the occasion. Sam had happily missed out on lunches to see her daughter looking so happy.

She regarded her daughter quizzically. 'You like him, don't you?'

Daisy nodded. 'He's nice.'

After spending the last twenty-four hours with him, that was even less the word Sam would have used to describe Xander Sterne than it had been when Daisy had asked about him yesterday afternoon!

He was impossible. Infuriating. Arrogant. Most certainly outrageous on occasion; Sam still hadn't forgotten that intimate conversation the previous evening regarding whether or not she had any tattoos, and where she might have them if she did. A tattoo that the scooped neckline of her gown barely managed to cover...

But *nice*? Xander was much too immediately male to be described with such an insipid word.

And yet Daisy, who was so often shy in the company of men, seemed totally relaxed in Xander's company.

Obviously Daisy saw something in him that Sam didn't.

Or, more likely, not...

Being only five, Daisy wouldn't be aware of Xander's immediacy, of how disturbingly *male* he was. Or recognise that the man possessed a lethal and sensual magnetism. And the naked body of a Norse god—

'Ready?'

And the stealth of a predator!

Sam had been so lost in her own thoughts that she hadn't even been aware of Xander's return, despite the sound the rubber end of his walking stick must surely have made on the marble floor.

She straightened her shoulders determinedly. 'Ready.' She nodded briskly. 'If you and Daisy would like to sit here and wait, I'll go down in the lift to the car park and bring your car round to the front of the building?' She looked down questioningly at Daisy.

'Good idea.' Xander nodded. 'We'll be okay here together, won't we, Daisy?' He hadn't missed Samantha's deference to her young daughter over the suggested arrangements.

Did Samantha somehow sense that inner rage Xander was at such pains to try and keep under his control?

He and Darius had found plenty of time to chat this morning, once Samantha had dropped him off at his brother's apartment. Darius had once again been at pains to reassure Xander that the reason for his rage six weeks ago was perfectly understandable, that *he* would have reacted to that situation in the same way, and that Xander had only responded so strongly to that situation because of their own family history of having an abusive father. That it didn't mean Xander would ever feel that angry again.

But what if Darius was wrong? And what if Samantha had sensed that rage inside him?

Xander gave a jolt of surprise as Daisy smiled up at him shyly as she slipped her warm little hand into his much larger one. 'I'll stay here and look after Xander for you, Mummy.'

Xander was so bemused by having that little hand resting so trustingly in his that it took him a second or two to register exactly what Daisy had said. Causing him to grimace, when he looked up to find himself the focus of the laughing eyes of Daisy's mother.

Great; not only was his blasted leg aching like the devil, because he had been on it for most of the day and had stubbornly refused to use his crutches, but now he was the focus of Daisy's sympathy and the butt of Samantha's amusement.

Still, there was some compensation to remaining here with Daisy, Xander decided as the two of them sat down in two of the armchairs in the marble reception area, and so allowing him to watch the sexy sway of Samantha's hips and bottom as she walked over to the lift that would take her down to the car parked in the underground car park, which he had insisted she use to drive herself and Daisy to the wedding earlier.

For all that she was only a little over five feet tall, Samantha's slender legs looked long and silky above the three-inch-heeled shoes she was wearing today.

Causing Xander to muse as to how it would feel to have those silky legs wrapped about his waist...

What the...?

While Xander had been sitting there imagining how he would make love to Samantha, another man had approached her and was now holding tightly to her arm as he talked to her.

A man, Xander noted grimly as Samantha turned briefly to shoot a worried glance in his own and Daisy's direction, who had caused her face to pale.

Xander instantly felt that rising tide of anger he had hoped never to feel again. And for the same reason: the sight of a man roughly manhandling a woman.

The man's fingers painfully gripped the top of one of Samantha's arms as he talked to her in a lowered and intense tone.

'Take your hand off me, Malcolm!' Sam snapped agitatedly as she stared up into the face of the man she had once been married to but had hoped never to set eyes on again after the divorce.

It was a handsome face still, dominated by glittering blue eyes, the darkness of Malcolm's hair, at the age of forty-one, showing only a distinguished sprinkling of grey at his temples, his perfectly tailored suit emphasising the width of his shoulders, and narrow waist and hips.

What were the chances, the probability, that Malcolm would be at the London Midas Hotel on the very same evening that Sam happened to be here for Andy and Darius's wedding reception?

What were the chances, with Sam's change in circumstances after their separation and divorce, that she would ever have been inside the exclusive Midas hotel at all, let alone on the same evening as her ex?

Unless...

Was it possible that Malcolm could be one of the evening guests invited to Andy and Darius's wedding?

Sam had mentioned her brief marriage and divorce to Andy, of course, but only in passing, and in relation to how that might affect Daisy. She certainly hadn't told her friend the name of the man she had once been briefly married to.

Sam knew the newly married couple had invited fifty or so guests for the evening part of the wedding reception, most of them parents of the children to whom Andy taught ballet, or business acquaintances of Darius's.

Was it possible that Malcolm was one of the latter?

It was more than possible, Sam acknowledged with an inward groan, wondering why it had never occurred to her before that Malcolm and Darius might know each other. Malcolm was a successful businessman, just as Darius and Xander were, and—

Did that mean that Xander knew Malcolm too?

'I asked what you're doing here, Sam,' Malcolm rasped harshly, her request that he release her obviously having had absolutely no effect, as his fingers continued to bite painfully into the top of her arm.

Her eyes flashed. 'And *I* told *you* that it's absolutely none of your business what I do any more.' She glanced behind him to where a beautiful blonde stood waiting for him.

'And aren't you being a little rude just leaving your date standing over there alone while you verbally abuse your ex-wife?'

'I don't give a damn whether it's rude or not.'

'Well, I do!' Sam snapped, her days of being intimidated by this man—visibly, at least— long over. Inwardly it was a different matter. Inwardly Malcolm still made her quake, but mainly with revulsion, she now realised with a frown. 'Take your hand off me, Malcolm, or I'll call someone over from hotel security and have them make you do it,' she warned coldly.

His face twisted viciously. 'Why, you little—'

'Now, Malcolm!' She met his furious gaze unflinchingly.

She wondered how she could ever have been married to this man. How she could ever have tried so hard to make that marriage work after Daisy was born. How she could ever have thought she *loved* him.

Oh, there was no doubting that Malcolm was still an attractive man, but Sam could now see and recognise the edge of cruelty to his mouth, and the cold calculation of those blue eyes that looked down at her so possessively.

'I think I like you like this, Sam.' Malcolm's gaze swept over her in blatant insolence. 'You look absolutely amazing in that red dress. Even better out of it, if my memory serves me correctly!'

Sam gave a shudder of revulsion as she recognised the flash of desire as Malcolm blatantly undressed her with his eyes.

'Lucky for me that I haven't forgotten a single thing about you!' she dismissed scornfully. 'Most especially how much I despise you!'

Malcolm's face flushed with fury. 'What have

you done with your precious daughter this evening while you're out enjoying yourself?'

It took every effort of will on Sam's part not to glance across the hotel reception to where Daisy sat beside Xander. The last thing she wanted was for Malcolm to realise that Daisy was here too, and possibly make even more of a scene in one of Xander's prestigious hotels.

Daisy hadn't so much as asked about her father once since the separation and divorce, and Sam doubted her daughter would even recognise him if she did see him. She *hoped and prayed* Daisy wouldn't recognise him.

She raised her chin. 'Again, Malcolm, that's absolutely none of your business.'

'She's my daughter too.'

'Daisy was never your daughter!' Sam hissed, her eyes flashing darkly as she felt absolutely incensed by Malcolm's claim. How dared he, after the way he had treated Daisy? How *dared* he? 'Get your hands off me now or I *will* call security.'

Malcolm regarded her through narrowed lids, that gleam of sexual admiration still glittering in his eyes as he slowly released her. 'How about I ditch my date for the evening and the two of us take a room here for the night instead?'

Sam drew in a harsh breath even as she gave another shiver of revulsion, wanting nothing more at that moment than to slap the man she had once been married to. 'Goodbye, Malcolm,' she said coldly instead, having just dared a glance across the reception area and seen that Xander was getting awkwardly to his feet, his tiredness making that more laborious than it might otherwise have been, while the darkness of his gaze was fixed steadily on where she and Malcolm stood in obviously heated conversation.

The last thing Sam wanted was for Xander to come over here and realise that she was talking to her ex-husband. An ex-husband he might possibly know too.

Bad enough that Sam and Malcolm had met again at all, but she knew Xander well enough to know he was the sort of man who would demand answers from her regarding the man who had spoken to her. That he would want details of the acquaintance. All of them.

They were details Sam didn't want to give him.

Mainly because she was too ashamed. Of how much, and for how long she had tried to make her marriage to Malcolm work, and the sacrifices she had made trying to achieve that.

Looking at Malcolm now, she was able to see beyond that surface charm and handsomeness that had once dazzled her into believing she was in love with him, as much as he claimed to be in love with her, and could now clearly recognise Malcolm's coldness, as well as his cruelty.

'Malcolm?' His date for the evening had obviously tired of waiting as she looked over at him in puzzled enquiry.

Malcolm turned to smile charmingly at the other woman. 'I'll be right there, Sonya.' His eyes hardened as he turned back to Sam. 'This conversation isn't over,' he warned her softly.

'Oh, it's most definitely over,' Sam assured him.

He smiled tauntingly. 'No, Sam, it really isn't.

I'm sure I'm going to find you so much more fun now that you're all grown up.'

Sam's eyes widened in alarm. 'We're divorced.'

'So?' he taunted. 'Never heard the phrase one more for the road?'

Surely that applied to a drink, and not—not—

'We have a deal,' she reminded shakily. 'Daisy and I will stay out of your life and you will stay out of ours.'

Malcolm gave an unconcerned shrug. 'And I'm willing to continue doing just that. For a price.'

'I already paid your price.'

'And now I'm going to collect the interest.' His eyes had narrowed darkly. 'Give my daughter a hug for me when you see her,' he added softly. Threateningly.

'You—'

'Enjoy the rest of your evening, Sam,' Malcolm taunted before turning on his heel to join his date for the evening, his hand beneath the other woman's elbow as the two of them then proceeded, as Sam had suspected that they might, towards the ballroom where Andy and Darius's wedding reception was being held.

Oh, why hadn't she left sooner? Why had she come here at all?

'Everything okay, Samantha?'

Sam was shaking so badly, her knees knocking so much, she wasn't sure she was going to be able to remain standing for much longer, let alone be capable of finding a suitable answer to Xander's puzzled query.

Was everything okay?

It couldn't have been less so.

Not only had Sam seen Malcolm again when she had been least expecting it, tonight or any other night, but he had definitely threatened her, and used a tacit threat against Daisy as leverage to cash in on it.

And the intelligent and astute Xander had been a witness to that meeting. Even if he could have no idea about the content of their conversation.

As for Daisy?

Sam looked down anxiously at her young daughter. She'd walked over with Xander, her hand still resting trustingly in his. Had Daisy recognised Malcolm as her father?

There was nothing in Daisy's face to indicate that she had. Her expression was one of tiredness rather than any sign of recognition for the man Sam had been talking to; Daisy's eyelids were drooping and her cheeks were slightly pale.

And really, why should Daisy recognise Malcolm? Her daughter hadn't even seen Malcolm since she was two years old, and only rarely before then.

'Who was that man, Samantha?'

She swallowed before answering. 'Just someone who obviously mistook me for someone else.' She shrugged dismissively.

Xander frowned. 'The conversation seemed rather protracted just for you to tell him he'd made a mistake in identity?'

Her mouth firmed stubbornly. 'Nevertheless, that's what I was doing. We might as well all go down in the lift to the car park together now that the two of you are right here?' she prompted lightly as the lift doors opened and she stepped inside to look at him enquiringly.

Xander had absolutely no doubt that Samantha was lying to him.

The intensity of the conversation he had witnessed, the expressions on Samantha's face as she spoke to the other man, certainly hadn't looked as if she was politely assuring a stranger that he had mistaken her for someone else. The opposite, in fact. Samantha had initially looked distressed, and then her expression had become coldly impenetrable, followed by one of fear. Xander had also recognised an almost proprietary gleam of ownership in the other man's eyes at one stage of that intense conversation.

Because the man felt proprietary in regard to Samantha? Perhaps because he was an ex-lover?

It was certainly a more plausible explanation for the heated encounter than the one Samantha had just given him.

That flare of temper Xander had felt—and so feared feeling again—when he first saw the guy manhandling Samantha had now settled into a deep-down coldness.

He still wanted to strangle the man, for daring to put his hand on Samantha, but it was in a cold and measured way, rather than down to a heated lack of control.

Whether or not that control would last was anyone's guess!

'Fine,' he agreed tersely to Samantha's suggestion as he and Daisy stepped into the lift beside her, deciding to let the conversation go. For now.

But he had every intention of making Samantha tell him the truth about the man who had accosted her.

And sooner rather than later.

'Daisy okay?' Xander enquired as Samantha hovered in the doorway of the sitting room after bathing her daughter and putting her to bed.

'Already fast asleep.' Samantha nodded. She'd changed into a thin blue sweater and faded jeans, her feet were bare, and her hair once again secured at her crown.

'Join me for a nightcap.' Xander held up a decanter of brandy, having removed his morning jacket and cravat, and unfastening the top button of his wing-collared white shirt. 'And before you even think about saying no thank you, in your oh-so-polite manner—' his voice hardened as he poured the brandy into two crystal glasses '—it wasn't a request.' He looked across at her challengingly.

Sam felt an uneasy lurch of her stomach as she recognised Xander's uncompromising expression. 'I'm tired.'

'It's only a little after ten o'clock.'

'And it's been a long and exciting day.'

'Then a brandy will help relax you before you go to bed.' He left his walking stick beside the fireplace as he limped slowly across the room to place the two glasses of brandy down on the coffee table before sinking down onto the cream leather sofa.

'I'm already relaxed.'

'Liar.' Xander could literally *feel* Samantha's tension, and he could see it too, in the way she held herself so stiffly.

She frowned. 'I don't think I care for the way you keep calling me that.'

His eyes flashed darkly. 'And I don't think *I* care for being lied to.'

Her mouth set in a stubborn line. 'Then maybe you should stop asking questions I obviously don't want to answer.'

Xander felt some of his rising tension leave him as he smiled ruefully. 'Now *that* was honest.'

She frowned. 'I am invariably honest. You just keep asking me questions that are none of your business, and then won't accept it when I refuse to answer them.'

'Would you please sit down and enjoy your brandy?' he invited huskily as he patted the leather seat cushion beside him.

Samantha walked further into the room, but she made no effort to sit beside him as she instead picked up one of the glasses of brandy from the coffee table and took a large swallow, only to then draw her breath in sharply as the fiery liquid caught the back of her throat.

'Whoa,' she gasped breathlessly, her cheeks becoming flushed, tears blurring her vision.

Xander chuckled softly. 'You're supposed to sip a fine brandy, Samantha, not glug it back like cheap wine.'

'And what would you know about cheap wine?' she scorned as she moved to sit in one of the armchairs, bending her legs at the knees before tucking her bare feet beneath her, the glass of brandy cradled in both her hands.

'Absolutely nothing,' he acknowledged dryly. 'So who was he, Samantha?'

'Who was who?' She tensed guardedly.

A very revealing guardedness and tension.

'The man at the hotel. Was he a past lover?' Xander pressed. 'Or maybe a current one, that you discovered was out on the town with another woman behind your back?'

'Don't be ridiculous!' she snapped crossly.

'Which part of what I said was ridiculous?' Xander raised his brows. 'The old lover or the new lover?'

'Both,' she dismissed. 'I don't have any old lovers, and I'm too busy working and being a mother to Daisy to have the time for any new ones either.'

Interesting…

Did that mean that Daisy's father had been the only man ever to share her bed? To touch every naked inch of her?

That seemed a little hard to believe when he knew that Samantha had been divorced for the past three years. Was she saying she also hadn't had sex with anyone for the past three years?

Xander didn't think he'd ever gone three months without a woman in his bed, let alone three years.

He looked across at her now through narrowed lids. 'How old are you?'

'I— What?' She looked nonplussed by the question.

'How old are you?' Xander repeated with a shrug. 'It's a simple enough question, I would have thought.'

Simple maybe, but Sam didn't see what her age had to do with anything, let alone their present—and deeply personal—conversation. 'How old are you?' she countered challengingly.

'Thirty-three,' he answered without hesitation.

That put Sam in the position of looking petty if she didn't reciprocate.

She sighed. 'I'm twenty-six.'

His brows rose. 'You must have been very young when you married?'

She grimaced. 'What does age have to do with anything when you fall in love?' Or *believe* you've fallen in love.

'I can't answer that, as I've never fallen in love.' Xander shrugged. 'That means you could only have been twenty-one when Daisy was born.'

'Yes.'

'And just twenty-three when you and your husband separated and then divorced?'

Sam felt her tension deepen as she wondered exactly where this conversation was going. 'Yes.'

'And you're saying that you haven't had sex even once since then? Not even with your ex-husband, for old times' sake?' Xander seemed to remember reading that a high percentage of separated couples did that.

Samantha's face paled, her hands shaking as she tightly gripped the glass of brandy. 'Don't be disgusting,' she finally managed to gasp.

Xander's eyes were narrowed as he gave a slow shake of his head. 'I don't buy the story you gave me earlier, Samantha. I believe you did know the man who spoke to you at the hotel. That you know him very well.'

'Did *you* know him?'

'Me?' Xander frowned as he brought an image of the man back into his head. 'I couldn't see his face properly, because he was turned away from me, but I didn't know him, that I'm aware of.' Although it was interesting that Sam had asked. 'I still think that you did, or still do, know him very well indeed.'

She sat forward to slam the bulbous brandy glass down onto the table beside her with such vehemence that some of the alcohol spilt over the rim of the crystal glass. 'How did we progress from me telling you I'm tired, to you accusing me of having once been intimate with some stranger I met in a hotel who mistook me for someone else?'

Considering Xander's misgivings these past months, in regard to his own temper, and his doubts in his ability to control it, Samantha really *did* look amazing when she was angry.

Everything about her seemed to spark with life: her hair, her eyes, that flush in her cheeks, a puffy fullness to her slightly parted lips, her nipples aroused and pressing against her bra and the thin jersey of her jumper.

'I don't know—how did we come to that?' Xander asked softly. 'Maybe if you were to stop ly— Maybe if you told me the truth,' he amended as Samantha looked ready to explode if he called her a liar one more time tonight, 'I wouldn't have to keep asking the same question but in a different format.'

'The question being who was the man at the hotel earlier?' she snapped impatiently.

'Yes.'

'I've told you, I don't—' Sam broke off her protest as the sound of a piercing scream filled the apartment.

'Daisy!' She sprang quickly to her feet, not sparing Xander a second glance as she fled from the room and down the hallway to her daughter's bedroom.

CHAPTER SIX

SAM HAD LEFT Daisy's door slightly ajar and a night light on, as she always did, and she quickly pushed the door fully open now before running across the room to where her daughter was sitting up in bed. Daisy's eyes were wide, the tears streaming down her feverishly flushed face as she continued to scream.

'I'm here, Daisy.' Sam sat on the side of the bed to take her daughter into her arms. 'It's okay, darling,' she soothed as her daughter struggled to be set free. 'It's Mummy, darling. It's Mummy, Daisy,' she repeated firmly as she stroked her daughter's hair back from her flushed face.

Daisy stopped struggling but still trembled as she now looked up uncertainly. 'Mummy?'

Sam smiled at her reassuringly. 'You had a bad dream, darling. Just a dream,' she soothed as Daisy, calmer now, snuggled against her for comfort.

At the same time Sam's thoughts were inwardly racing. Had Daisy recognised Malcolm at the hotel earlier, after all? Either consciously, or subconsciously? And was that the reason for her daughter's nightmare?

It was like one of those night terrors that Daisy had suffered from as a very young child, but she hadn't had a single one in the past three years. Not since they'd left Malcolm.

'Is she okay?'

Sam turned sharply to look at Xander as he quietly entered the bedroom, an anxious frown on her face as she wondered how Daisy would react to the presence of a man in her bedroom so soon after her nightmare.

'Xander!' Daisy pulled out of Sam's arms before launching herself off the bed towards him.

Giving Sam a very definitive answer to that question.

Xander only just managed to open his arms in time to the little girl. As it was, he had to drop his walking stick on the floor, swaying precariously for several seconds as his injured leg threatened to collapse beneath him. Daisy might only be a lightweight, but her sudden weightfirm grasp on his leg caused a jolt of pain from Xander's thigh down to his knee.

Xander glanced at Samantha, noting the pallor of her cheeks, and the tears glistening in her shadowed eyes, her expression dazed, lost, as she sat on Daisy's bed looking at them both. Had there been something more sinister to Daisy's nightmare than that the little girl had simply had an over-stimulating day?

Daisy gave a yawn as she nestled against him and he slowly led her back to the bed.

Within seconds of her lying down, it seemed, the little girl had fallen back to sleep, as if the nightmare had never occurred or woken her up screaming. Chances were—Xander hoped— that Daisy wouldn't even remember she'd had the nightmare in the morning.

Her mother looked far less composed, Xander noted. Samantha's expression was still one of devastation, her face drawn and pale, shadows having deepened in those beautiful eyes.

'Let's go and finish our brandy,' Xander encouraged, wincing slightly as he straightened from picking his cane up from the bedroom floor.

'Maybe I should stay here for a while, just in case?' Samantha looked worriedly at her sleeping daughter.

'We'll hear her if she calls out again.' Xander held his hand out to Samantha as encouragement for her to stand up and leave the bedroom with him. It was the most he could manage, his leg now a painful and throbbing ache. 'Come on, Samantha,' he encouraged gruffly, knowing he badly needed to sit down.

Sam looked up at him blankly, too disturbed still by Daisy's nightmare to be able to respond.

Nightmares had been a regular occurrence when Daisy was much younger, and at the time Sam hadn't equated them with the tension of living with Malcolm. She had only realised that significance when they had abruptly stopped once she and Daisy had moved out of Malcolm's house and begun living on their own.

Until tonight.

It was too much of a coincidence, surely, that this should have happened after seeing Malcolm at the hotel earlier?

Admittedly Daisy had given no indication at the time that she had recognised her father, but maybe it hadn't been a conscious recognition but a subliminal one? The mind often played strange tricks on people, so maybe Daisy *had* recognised Malcolm without even being aware that she had?

'Samantha?' Xander asked again gently.

She blinked, focusing on him with effort. 'Sorry.' She grimaced, giving herself a mental shake as she stood up. 'That was…unexpected,' she murmured as she followed him from the bedroom, leaving the door wide open this time, the better to be able to hear Daisy if she should call out again.

'Just over-excitement, do you think?' Xander wondered, replenishing their brandy glasses once they had returned to the sitting room, before handing one to Samantha. 'You'll feel better if you drink some more of that,' he encouraged gruffly. 'Slowly this time.'

Sam obediently took the glass from him, still worried about Daisy's nightmare, and not in the mood to argue with Xander over a glass of brandy. 'It was a different sort of day for her, with lots of unusual, if exciting, stimuli,' she answered him woodenly.

'But?' Xander observed her closely as he moved to sink down onto the sofa.

Because he really did think he was now in danger of falling down.

And wouldn't that look just wonderful, very manly, if he were to keel over and collapse at Samantha's bare feet?

His leg was giving him hell, after he had been on it for so many hours already today, and it hadn't helped when Daisy had launched herself at him just now when he hadn't been expecting it.

Although physically painful, having Daisy turn to him in that way for reassurance and comfort had surprisingly felt quite nice.

To know that Daisy liked him enough, trusted him enough, to want to turn to him for comfort was a good feeling after Xander's weeks of uncertainty about himself.

It made him even more determined to be worthy of Daisy's trust.

Samantha looked as if she was in need of a little comfort too right now.

'Come and sit beside me,' he instructed in a voice that brooked no argument. 'Don't make me have to stand up again and come get you, Samantha,' he added with a pained wince.

She looked at him blankly again for several long seconds, almost as if she had forgotten he was there, before moving stiffly across the room to sit down beside him.

Maybe she really had forgotten he was there?

Surely children of all ages had nightmares? A result of a too-active imagination at that age? Xander seemed to remember having them as a child himself. Of course, his had been due to living with his bastard of a father, but—

His gaze sharpened on Samantha as he once again took in the pallor of her cheeks, and those dark shadows in her unusual amethyst-coloured eyes.

He recalled the sense he'd had earlier that she was lying to him…

'The man at the hotel…' he spoke softly now '…he was your ex-husband, wasn't he?' It was a statement rather than a question. Because Xander didn't need to ask the question when he already knew, instinctively, that he had guessed correctly.

The man who had accosted Samantha at the hotel, and taken such a painful grip of her arm, causing her face to pale as he spoke to her so intensely, was Samantha's ex-husband, and Daisy's father.

Sam turned on the sofa to look at Xander, intending to deny the statement, only to think better of it as she saw the implacability of his expression, and the challenge in the darkness of his eyes. As if he expected her to deny it, and was silently warning her against even trying.

She drew in a deep and ragged breath before answering him.

'Yes,' she sighed. 'Yes, he was,' she repeated, her shoulders slumping as she sank back against the sofa, head resting back as she closed her eyes. 'It was— I— It was such a shock because I haven't set eyes on him for almost three years.'

'Until tonight.'

'Until tonight.' She nodded.

'It didn't look as if it was a joyful reunion?'

Sam didn't open her eyes. 'Not exactly the highlight of my day, no.'

'Well of course not—that was coming into the church earlier and seeing how handsome I looked in my morning suit!'

Sam opened one eye as she turned her head to look at Xander seated beside her, receiving a cheeky smile for her effort. 'Your modesty is just overwhelming!' she drawled as she closed her eye again.

It didn't help that Xander *had* looked gorgeous in his morning suit. Or that Sam's heart *had* given a lurch as she had gazed down the aisle on her arrival at the church, and seen him sitting at the front, looking as handsome and golden as that Norse god he so resembled.

The Sterne twins had made such a contrast as they'd stood up together at the sound of the

Wedding March playing to announce Andy's arrival outside the church, Darius so dark and compelling, Xander all mesmerising light.

'Isn't it?' Xander teased lightly, relieved to see the smile now curving the fullness of Samantha's lips, even if it was being forced for his benefit.

Full and delectable lips that Xander had wanted to kiss since the moment he saw her in that red dress as she walked into the church earlier today.

His thoughts drifted back to the hotel earlier, and what he had been able to see of the man he now knew to be Samantha's ex-husband. He had been tall in an expensively tailored dark suit, his face strong in profile, dark hair peppered with silver at the temples. He must have been some years older than Samantha.

But what did it matter what he looked like or how old he was, when Samantha claimed the man had been out of the picture, out of her life, for the past three years?

And out of Daisy's, too?

Xander turned on the sofa, his thigh now

gently touching the length of hers. 'How does Daisy visit her father if you haven't seen your ex-husband for three years?'

Her mouth twisted. 'She doesn't.'

Xander frowned. 'But—'

'I don't want to talk about this any more tonight, Xander, okay?' Samantha snapped as she sat forward with the obvious intention of standing up.

'No, it's not okay.' Xander put his hand on her shoulder to prevent her from standing up. 'I want to understand, Samantha. I need to understand.'

'Why?'

'Because for some unknown reason I care!'

She gave a shake of her head. 'You don't even know me.'

'But I'm trying to.'

Samantha looked at him for several long seconds before giving a shake of her head. 'No. I—I can't do this.' Once again she attempted to stand up.

Unacceptable.

Totally unacceptable.

Samantha might not want to answer his questions right now, but that didn't change the desire Xander had felt all day to take this woman in his arms and kiss her. And now he wanted to keep on kissing her, until Samantha could think of nothing and no one else but him.

Was that even wise on his part, when the two of them were going to be living here together for the next two weeks?

After all the upsets Samantha had already been through today?

Oh, to hell with what was wise!

Xander *needed* to kiss Samantha, more than he wanted to breathe, and as much as he wanted to eliminate the sadness from her lips and those deep shadows from her eyes. 'Let me in, Samantha,' he groaned achingly as he moved closer to her.

Sam's eyes widened as Xander's face began to lower towards hers, the arm draped across the back of the sofa now dropping lightly down onto her shoulders, as she realised he was about to kiss her.

'Xander—' Her weak protest was cut short

as Xander's lips claimed hers in a gentle exploratory kiss.

Her heart leapt in her chest at the first touch of those sensually sculpted lips against her own, her hand seeming to move up of its own volition to cup Xander's slightly bristly cheek as he deepened the kiss, caressing and tasting, his arms moving about her waist as he pulled her body in close against him.

Sam had no resistance to those heated kisses, each more passionate than the last, the desire thrumming hotly through her body as she pressed her breasts against Xander's chest in an effort to try and ease some of the ache in her sensitive nipples.

Her breath caught in her throat as Xander's tongue now swept inside the heat of her mouth, with all the assurance of a Viking invader laying claim to his prize.

Xander gave a groan as he pressed Samantha gently back, until she lay beneath him on the sofa, her breasts warm and soft against the hardness of his chest, his legs becoming entangled with hers as they lay together, the evidence of his arousal a throbbing ache between them.

He murmured his pleasure as he felt Samantha's fingers in his hair as his lips now trailed across the warmth of her cheek and down the column of her throat, teeth nipping lightly on the lobe of her ear, causing her to moan huskily.

His lips moved lower, exploring the shadowed hollows at the base of her silky throat, one of his hands moving beneath her sweater against the heat of her skin. Samantha groaned low in her throat as one of his hands cupped her breast, its fullness filling his palm.

It was Xander's turn to groan as he felt the turgid heat of her nipple pressing against the material of her bra. He pushed her sweater up and out of the way as his lips trailed down to kiss the bared slopes of her breasts before unfastening her bra. He raised his head so that he could look down at her deliciously bared breasts.

Completely bared breasts that revealed the tattoo of an eagle soaring on the upper slope of her left breast.

'I knew it,' Xander groaned achingly even as he lowered his head and his tongue traced the outline of that utterly sexy tattoo.

He immediately realised his mistake in having spoken, as he felt Samantha tense and still beneath him, her fingers tightening briefly in his hair before moving down to his chest as she began to push him away.

'Please, Xander,' she groaned when he didn't move. 'You have to stop now!'

'Why do I?' he murmured distractedly as he continued to gaze down at those perfect breasts, tipped by swollen and aroused nipples. He was too turned on, too lost to the pleasure that was Samantha, to want to stop this just yet.

'Xander, please!' Her tone was more urgent now. 'I don't— We can't do this.' A sob caught in her throat as she pushed against his chest in earnest.

The haze of desire was slow to lift inside Xander's head, and it took him several seconds to realise that Samantha was pushing against him.

His head lifted slowly as he looked at her, those perfect rounded breasts quickly rising and falling as she breathed heavily, her cheeks pale, her kiss-swollen lips parted, and her eyes wide pools of anguish.

Anguish?

Because Xander had kissed and caressed her? Kisses and caresses she had seemed to enjoy? Seemed…

Could Xander be wrong about Samantha's response? Could he have wanted to kiss and touch her so much that he had mistaken her initial lack of protest as encouragement?

Was it possible that it had been so long since he last spent any time with a woman, held a woman in his arms, that he had misread the signals? That he was so physically frustrated he was guilty of kissing the first woman who had seemed willing?

Well, that last bit wasn't true, at least; the bridesmaid at the wedding had been more than willing to share his bed tonight. Hell, she had been more than willing for them to book into a room at the hotel for the night!

She just hadn't been the woman that Xander wanted.

Because the woman now lying beneath him was the woman he wanted. Samantha Smith. Mother to Daisy Smith.

And the ex-wife of the man who had upset her earlier at the hotel…

Damn it, *of course* he had misread the signals!

Samantha hadn't been inviting him to kiss her just now. He had seen it himself; she had been in need of comfort after being so suddenly, so unexpectedly, confronted by her ex-husband. And then her daughter had woken screaming from a nightmare. A nightmare that had caused Daisy to turn to him for that same comfort.

Xander lifted himself up and away from Samantha before standing up, instantly wincing as the aching pain intensified in his leg. 'I'm sorry.' He ran an agitated hand through the heavy thickness of his hair.

The same hair that Samantha had tugged and pulled on a short time ago as she'd returned— when he had *thought* she'd returned—the heat of his kisses. Hell, maybe she had been trying to push him away even then!

Xander turned away from the guilt he felt just looking at Samantha as she refastened her bra and straightened her sweater before sitting upright on the sofa, her eyes dark and bruised-looking, her lips puffy from their kisses. 'I'm sorry,' he repeated abruptly. '*That* really was inappropriate of me.'

Sam knew it had been.

But oh, how she wished she hadn't needed to stop their kisses but could instead have taken what Xander had so obviously been offering: a night of uncomplicated and passionate sex.

Except it wouldn't be uncomplicated, not when Xander was the man she wanted to make love with, rather than her ex-husband who was demanding she go to bed with him again. Just thinking about Malcolm's threats earlier was enough to give *her* nightmares!

But her problems had nothing to do with Xander. The only reason she was staying in his apartment at all was to take care of him.

This was a *job,* for goodness' sake.

A job that certainly didn't come with the fringe benefit of sleeping with the boss.

Thank goodness Xander had spoken to her and broken the sensual spell she had fallen under, reminding her of where she was. Who she was with!

She was just so aware of his lethal attraction. The desire he had aroused in her that she had thought long dead.

But it wasn't only that. She was just as drawn to knowing the reasons behind those dark shadows that she occasionally saw lurking in the depths of his eyes. As if he had his own painful memories he had to deal with on a daily basis. Memories Sam wanted to know, and possibly share with him.

Which was utterly ridiculous.

Why on earth would Xander Sterne, billionaire playboy, have any painful memories, let alone want to share them with someone like her?

Admittedly his father had died when Xander was still quite young, which must have been difficult for him, but other than that he had led a charmed life. He was rich as Croesus, was obviously loved by his twin and his mother and stepfather. And, if the bridesmaid from earlier was any example, then women were obviously falling over themselves just to be with him.

So why on earth would he ever feel anything more than a fleeting attraction towards her, let alone a need to share any of his private life with the woman hired to take care of him while his brother was away on his honeymoon?

He wouldn't, came the unequivocal answer.

Even if there was something to share. Which there so obviously wasn't.

'I *am* sorry, Samantha.'

She didn't look at Xander as she nodded abruptly. 'So am I.'

'What do you have to be sorry about?'

A desire that had shocked her to her core.

Acknowledging Xander's lethal attraction and acting upon it were two distinctly different things, when Sam hadn't so much as looked at a man with interest since the end of her marriage to Malcolm. Even without Malcolm's threats earlier this evening, her ex-husband's unreasonable behaviour during their marriage should have been a stark lesson to her never to be fooled again by a good-looking face and a charming manner.

Tonight she had definitely returned the hunger of Xander's kisses. And allowed Xander to touch her more intimately than any other man had but her husband. She'd also been aroused in a way she could never remember being aroused before. Not even at the start of her marriage to Malcolm, the man she had believed herself to be in love with…

And that knowledge now terrified her!

She didn't want to feel anything for Xander Sterne beyond the necessary concern of a carer for her charge. She didn't want to like him. Or desire him. She certainly didn't want to ever be stupid enough to fall in love with him!

'Go to bed, Samantha,' Xander bit out harshly as he saw the way her face had now paled. 'I'll manage to undress myself this evening and you can help me shower in the morning,' he assured her dryly as she looked at him questioningly.

Her expression was noticeably one of relief. 'Are you sure?'

'Very,' Xander confirmed as Samantha rushed from the room.

Or a lustful Xander Sterne...

CHAPTER SEVEN

'GET IN THE CAR, Sam!'

It was such a pleasant sunny Monday morning that Sam had decided to walk Daisy to school, before leaving her daughter safely in her classroom.

Despite Malcolm's threats on Saturday night—threats Sam had been trying to forget all weekend—she was completely unprepared, as she left the school grounds, to see Malcolm sitting behind the wheel of the sleek black saloon car, the passenger-seat window lowered so that he could speak to her.

Sam desperately tried to gather her scattered wits together as she glared into the open window at him. She didn't fool herself for a moment that this was going to be any more pleasant a meeting than the one on Saturday evening had been.

Malcolm's eyes narrowed to blue chips of ice as she made no move to do as he instructed. 'Get in the damned car, Sam,' he repeated harshly. 'Unless you would prefer I get out of the car and we talk right there on the pavement?' he added challengingly, as several of the other mothers leaving the school gave them obviously curious looks as they walked past them.

Unsurprisingly, when for the last eight months Sam had always been alone when she delivered and collected Daisy from school.

'What are you even doing here, Malcolm?' she demanded as she wrenched the car door open and slid into the passenger seat beside him, knowing she had no other choice if she didn't want to cause a scene. And for Daisy's sake, she really didn't.

Her one defiant gesture was to deliberately slam the car door shut. She knew how it would irritate Malcolm; unlike his behaviour towards his wife and daughter, Malcolm had always been obsessive about the care and treatment of his cars.

Shut in the confines of the vehicle with him,

Sam instantly became aware of the spicy—and expensive—aftershave Malcolm had always worn, and which she had only ever associated with him. To a degree that if she had happened to smell it randomly these past three years, on some other man, it had always made her feel slightly nauseous. As it now caused her to swallow down the bile rising in her throat.

Goodness knew the rest of her weekend had been awkward enough, without this.

There had been Malcolm's horrible threats for her to deal with, and on top of that Sam had been dreading seeing Xander again on Sunday morning after the intimacies of the previous evening.

But she needn't have worried about the latter, because Xander obviously regretted that lapse as much as she did. The two of them had barely exchanged half a dozen words as she'd helped him in and then out of the shower yesterday morning. Later he had refused her polite invitation for him to join her and Daisy when they went swimming an hour or so after lunch. And he had been secluded in his study working when the two of them returned to the apartment, assuring Sam he would get himself a snack to eat later in the evening if he felt hungry.

If he had done so then Sam had been fast asleep in her bed when it happened.

The only positive thing about yesterday had been that Daisy had seemed completely unaware that she'd had a nightmare the previous night. Nor had there been a repeat of it last night, thank goodness.

Sam looked at Malcolm warily. 'I wasn't even aware you knew where Daisy went to school.'

He gave her a satisfied smile. 'You might be surprised at what I've been able to find out about you and Daisy in the past twenty-four hours.'

She gasped. 'Have you had someone spying on me?'

That smile faded as he now looked at her with icy eyes through narrowed lids. 'I had no idea I needed to until I saw you at the Midas Hotel on Saturday evening,' he dismissed harshly.

Sam's heart sank at the mention of that meeting and Malcolm's threats to her.

Malcolm's mouth thinned. 'I hired a private investigator, and guess what he's already found out? My ex-wife and my daughter are currently living with Xander Sterne in his apartment.' His eyes glittered darkly.

Colour warmed Sam's previously pale cheeks. 'It's none of your business where we live, Malcolm.'

'I'm making it my business, Sam!' Malcolm reached out to take a painful grip of her wrist. 'Xander Sterne!' He gave a disbelieving shake of his head.

She struggled to free herself. 'Let go of me!' she ordered when Malcolm's fingers tightened more painfully.

He gritted his teeth. 'You obviously have a thing about rich and powerful men,' he taunted.

'If you mean that I despise them, then yes I do.'

'The fact you're living with Sterne would seem to contradict that statement.'

Sam gave an inward shiver at the cold fury

she could now see in Malcolm's eyes. 'I am not romantically involved with Mr Sterne.'

'My information says you are,' Malcolm rasped. 'And you've dragged my daughter into your little affair,' he continued purposefully. 'I think that might be grounds for bringing your fitness as a mother into question.'

'How dare you?' Sam rounded on him furiously, breathing hard in her agitation. 'How dare you even say that to me after— *You're* the one who has always refused to acknowledge her existence! The one who *sold* his daughter in exchange for my not asking for a divorce settlement, which would have enabled me to stay at home and be a full-time mother to Daisy. How dare you now accuse me of being an unfit mother, when you have never been a father to Daisy, even for a minute?' She glowered at him.

He shrugged broad shoulders. 'Maybe I've changed? Maybe I realise it's time I got to know my daughter better? I'm sure the courts would lend a sympathetic ear if I were to—'

'No!' Sam protested fiercely at the threat. 'I won't allow it. I won't allow *you* anywhere near— We had a deal!' she accused heatedly. 'No divorce settlement for me in exchange for full custody of Daisy.'

'And as I said to you on Saturday evening, there's absolutely no reason why that can't continue,' he came back softly. 'Once you've ditched Sterne and become my mistress, of course.'

Sam stared at him in complete horror, feeling as if her feet had been knocked from underneath her. 'I won't—I can't!'

'But you will,' Malcolm insisted. 'For Daisy's sake, you know you will.'

Sam looked at him searchingly, once again able to see that cruelty in Malcolm's eyes and in the harsh slashes beside his nose and mouth. She wanted Daisy to have nothing to do with this man. Being her daughter's biological father didn't make Malcolm any less the cruel and controlling man he had always been beneath that outward layer of social charm. There was no telling what damage Malcolm might do to Daisy emotionally if he were to obtain weekly visiting rights with her.

'Why are you doing this, Malcolm?' she prompted emotionally, knowing she was on the verge of tears. And she really didn't want to give Malcolm the satisfaction of reducing her to tears, when he must already be aware, by the hold he had of her wrist, how badly she was shaking. *'Why?'*

'Obviously because I've decided that I want you back in my bed.' He shrugged.

Sam stared at him dazedly. 'I don't love you, Malcolm. I don't even like you!'

'What has that got to do with anything?' He looked at her pityingly. 'The thing is, Sam, I really don't like the idea of you belonging to any other man but me. I realised when I saw you again the other night that what's mine should stay mine.'

'I don't *belong* to anyone, Malcolm.'

'Not for the past three years you haven't, no.' Malcolm confirmed that he really had had her investigated. 'And you aren't going to belong to anyone else now, either. So I suggest that you and Daisy move out of Sterne's apartment as soon as you've told him your little affair is over. Preferably before the end of the week,' Malcolm bit out.

Sam frowned. 'I can't do that.'

'That's a pity.' His tone was deceptively mild.

And Sam wasn't deceived for a moment. 'You don't understand,' she came back agitatedly. 'I don't *live* with Xander Sterne, I work for him. As his carer,' she added impatiently as Malcolm eyed her sceptically. 'He was involved in a car accident, and now needs help to—to—' Somehow Sam didn't think it was a good idea to tell Malcolm that one of the things she did for Xander was to help him in and out of the shower! 'I cook for him and help him when necessary,' she substituted.

Talking of which, it was almost time for her to drive Xander to his physiotherapy session as Paul had the day off.

'And those *duties* include you sleeping with him too?'

'You're wrong!' Embarrassed colour heated her cheeks as she recalled how close she had come to doing exactly that on Saturday night.

A guilty blush which caused Malcolm's eyes

to narrow dangerously. 'Even if what you say is true, you aren't seriously expecting me to believe that Xander Sterne has a beautiful woman living in his apartment with him, but that he hasn't slept with her yet?'

'That's exactly what I'm telling you,' Sam maintained stubbornly.

'And there's no yet about it,' she added firmly. 'I'm only staying at his apartment for a couple of weeks,' she insisted. 'Just until his brother returns from his honeymoon. You were at the wedding on Saturday, too, so you know I'm telling the truth.'

'About Darius being away on his honeymoon, at least, yes.' He nodded. '*If* what you say is true—'

'It is.'

'Then it won't be difficult to find someone else to take care of him while his brother is away so that you can move out in the next few days.'

Not difficult at all, which was why Sam was so grateful to have this job at all; the Sterne family could have employed anyone to care for

Xander, but they had chosen her, Andy had chosen her.

'I can't do that,' she insisted, knowing she couldn't let Andy down, or forget the fact that the money she earned these two weeks would pay her bills.

Malcolm now eyed her thoughtfully. 'You've changed, Sam; once upon a time you wouldn't have dreamt of answering me back.'

'Once upon a time I was stupid enough to think myself in love with you, too!' she replied heatedly, knowing she shouldn't antagonise Malcolm in the circumstances, but totally unable to stop herself from retaliating to that last jibe.

His mouth twisted into the semblance of a smile. 'But not any longer.'

'That's one of the reasons we're divorced, remember?' Sam eyed him warily.

'I remember only too well.' Malcolm's mouth thinned. 'I have never liked failure, Sam. And I definitely consider my marriage to you to be in that category.'

She gave a pained frown. 'And whose fault

was that? If you had told me you didn't want children then I would never have married you in the first place.' Having long been an orphan, Sam had always wanted children of her own. She hadn't just wanted children, she had *ached* for a family of her own, to love and care for, and to be loved and cared for in return. Instead she had got Malcolm.

And Daisy…

Daisy made up for all the pain, all the disillusionment of those unhappy years of being married to a man as cold and controlling as her ex-husband.

She would do anything to protect Daisy.

Anything at all.

'I want you back in my bed, Sam, and I think you know me well enough to know that I'll use any means at my disposal to achieve that,' Malcolm informed her confidently.

Almost as if he had been able to read her thoughts.

And maybe he had. Malcolm already knew that Daisy was Sam's weak spot, her Achilles heel. And now he was once again using that weakness to his advantage, in an effort to force her into resuming a relationship with him. A relationship that horrified Sam so much she felt physically ill.

'No,' she answered him woodenly.

He arched mocking brows. 'No?'

'No,' she repeated firmly.

She had thought about this all weekend, finally accepting that she couldn't allow herself to be browbeaten by Malcolm again, to be forced into becoming his mistress. She just couldn't!

There had to be some other way. Some way to stop his blackmail once and for all. There just had to be.

'And if I insist?'

Sam was breathing hard, her emotions in turmoil. But she couldn't, she wouldn't, give in to Malcolm's blackmail. Because she knew that once it started it would never stop. Until one day she would wake up and find herself once again imprisoned, totally entrapped.

She drew herself up determinedly. 'You can

insist all you like, Malcolm, but my answer will still be no.'

He shrugged, his fingers once again tightening painfully about her wrist. 'Obviously you would rather the two of us talked through our lawyers.'

'I would *rather*—' She broke off, her eyes stinging with unshed tears, knowing she had to get away, before she gave Malcolm the satisfaction of seeing those tears fall. 'I have nothing more to say to you, Malcolm. And I have to go now,' she added before he could speak again. 'I have to drive Mr Sterne to his physio appointment.'

'Have dinner with me this evening, Sam, and we can discuss this further then.'

Sam repressed a shiver of fear. 'I'm not going to do this, Malcolm,' she told him shakily. 'Not dinner this evening, not any of it.'

He chuckled softly. 'Give it time, Sam, and you'll do exactly as I want,' he drawled confidently. 'You have until the end of the week,' he added coldly. 'After which I'm calling my lawyer.'

Sam wrenched her wrist painfully from his grasp before opening the car door and climbing quickly out onto the pavement, slamming the door closed behind her, before turning on her heel and walking off in the direction of Xander's apartment.

All the time aware that her wrist ached abominably, her knees were knocking together, and her body was shaking in complete awareness of the fact that Malcolm had just demanded that she become his mistress by threatening Daisy.

A demand, despite her defiance of him, that placed her as the fly to Malcolm's spider...

Xander had been aware that there was something seriously wrong with Samantha from the moment she'd returned from walking Daisy to school earlier that morning. Her face was pale, her eyes almost feverish, and she was totally distracted as she went off to change into a red long-sleeved shirt before silently driving him to his physio appointment. The return journey had been made just as quietly.

Xander was thoroughly worried by her un-characteristic silence by the time they arrived back at his apartment just before one o'clock, and he now sat at the breakfast bar watching her as she moved about the kitchen preparing lunch. 'Are you still angry with me for what happened on Saturday evening?' he finally prompted gruffly.

Events that had resulted in him spending two sleepless nights unable to banish thoughts of Samantha, who was lying in her own bed just a short distance down the hallway. He had won-dered if she was also awake and thinking of him.

Somehow Xander doubted that very much.

Samantha had been so cool towards him on Sunday, so businesslike in her dealings with him today, even when helping him in and out of the shower this morning. An occasion when he had been unable to hide the arousal her touch incited in him. He might as well have been a block of wood for all the notice Samantha had taken of that!

And that rankled.

This whole indifference thing Samantha now had going towards him rankled!

Okay, so he had read the signs wrong on Saturday evening, had realised almost immediately that he should have offered her comfort, with his arms and words, rather than kissing her. He was also aware he wasn't feeling his best right now. His leg was still aching badly from all the extra activity on Saturday; the wedding, Daisy throwing herself at him, *kissing Samantha*. But he had never had a woman react towards him with such indifference as Samantha had been doing these past two days and nights.

Maybe he was losing his touch?

And maybe Samantha would just rather forget those kisses had ever happened?

Wouldn't that be a dent to his already bruised ego?

'What?' She turned to look at him blankly now, almost as if she had forgotten he was there for a moment, colour suffusing her cheeks as his words penetrated her thoughts. 'Not in the least,' she dismissed, her head now buried in the refrigerator. 'I'd forgotten about it.'

Her sudden blush seemed to indicate that it really had been the last thing on her mind.

Oh, she hadn't forgotten about it yesterday, had been very skittish towards him over breakfast, so much so that Xander had decided it would be better if the two of them avoided each other's company for the rest of the day, especially in front of Daisy.

But here and now? Yes, Xander could well believe that this Samantha had completely forgotten about the two of them kissing on Saturday night. The question was, what had happened since yesterday—since breakfast this morning, in fact—to cause Samantha to be so distracted that she wasn't even defending herself? It was very unlike her.

'Do you want ham or cheese for your sandwich?' she asked distractedly now.

'Both,' Xander answered her just as dismissively. 'Samantha?'

'In that case, your lunch is ready,' she announced briskly.

Xander glanced down at the breakfast bar, his

eyes narrowing as he saw that only one place had been laid. 'Aren't you eating too?'

'I'm not hungry.'

'You only had coffee for breakfast.'

'Are you spying on me, too?' She glared at him accusingly. 'Because if you are, I advise you to stop. Right now!' She was trembling with anger.

'Whoa, Samantha.' Xander reached out with both arms to grasp her about the waist as she would have turned and marched angrily from the room, his leg giving a protesting jolt of pain as he did so. Xander ignored that pain as he instead looked down searchingly into Samantha's face; her eyes still sparkled with that earlier temper, her cheeks were flushed with anger, her mouth—her mouth…!

Xander was breathing hard as he gazed down at that perfect, tempting bow, the bottom lip fuller than the top. These were the lips that had haunted him day and night these past two days. And right now those delicious lips were as red and plump as ripe berries, no doubt caused by that same flush of anger.

Why was Samantha so angry? It seemed completely out of context to their conversation.

'What did you mean when you said *too*?' Xander asked, his eyes narrowing suspiciously. 'Who else has been spying on you, Samantha?' he prompted.

Sam's anger left her as quickly as it had arisen as she realised her mistake. Xander was just too intelligent, too astute, not to have noted and questioned her earlier comment. Or to add two and two together and not to come up with the right answer. If not now, then at some later time.

Xander hadn't recognised Malcolm on Saturday, and a part of Sam didn't want Xander to know that she had once been married to a man like Malcolm Howard, let alone that he was now threatening her.

She trembled every time she thought of her earlier conversation with Malcolm—which had been often in the past few hours! She knew she couldn't allow Malcolm to come even close to demanding visiting rights with Daisy.

Which meant what?

That she would have to telephone Malcolm and agree to have dinner with him this evening, at least?

Sam hated the thought of even doing that, let alone agreeing to Malcolm's other demands.

But she knew Malcolm too well, knew how clever he was at pretence, how charming he could be, and how easily he would be able to fool a judge into believing he was totally contrite regarding his previous attitude towards his daughter, and that he now wanted the chance to become a father to her.

Daisy would be totally bewildered by suddenly having a father she had never known thrust into her life. Her daughter would be hurt and confused. Miserable. And Sam would be just as miserable, but also worried out of her mind on those occasions when Malcolm was allowed to take Daisy out. It simply couldn't be allowed to happen.

She looked up at Xander. 'Would you please release me?'

Xander looked down at her searchingly, totally unsettled by the look of pained resolve in her eyes. As if she had come to a decision she didn't like. A decision she hated, if the grey tinge to her cheeks was any indication.

His mouth thinned. 'Answer my question, Samantha.'

'Release me now, Xander.' She challenged him as she pulled out of his arms.

Leaving Xander with no choice but to reach out and grasp hold of the breakfast bar in an effort to stop himself from overbalancing and toppling over, at the same time as he reached out with the other hand to fold the length of his fingers about Samantha's wrist to prevent her from moving any further away from him.

Samantha's gasp of pain was the last reaction Xander was expecting to so light a physical touch. 'What's wrong?' He scowled darkly as he lifted her arm and saw the bandage wrapped about her wrist, previously concealed beneath the long-sleeved red shirt she had changed into after taking Daisy to school. 'What happened to your wrist?' he demanded. 'Did you cut yourself? Sprain your wrist? Tell me how you did this, Samantha.'

'Or what? Will you *make* me tell you, Xander?' she added scornfully. 'Refuse to release me until I do?'

All of the above, as far as Xander was concerned, because he was not allowing Samantha to leave this kitchen until he knew exactly what was going on with her. Because something most certainly was!

Except…

He could see by Samantha's almost resigned expression that she was expecting him to bully her into giving him an answer.

Xander might be guilty of a lot of things—might now be living in fear of his temper allowing him to do even worse things—but bullying a woman, in any way, certainly wasn't one of them.

He maintained a light hold on Samantha's arm as his thoughts drifted back to this morning. She had seemed quiet but cheerful enough when she'd made them all breakfast. Her mood had only changed to one of complete introspection after she'd returned from taking Daisy to school. The same time that she had changed into the long-sleeved shirt.

Xander's eyes narrowed purposefully as he lifted that wrist before folding back some of the elasticated bandage to reveal the multicoloured bruising beneath.

Samantha immediately attempted to snatch her wrist out of his grasp. 'Don't!'

'Who did this?' Xander demanded with icy intensity, a red tide of anger washing over him as he recognised the bruises about the delicacy of Samantha's wrist as being in the pattern of fingerprints. A man's larger fingerprints, if he wasn't mistaken. 'Who did this to you, Samantha?' he demanded harshly.

Tears glistened in her eyes, her lashes blinking, and her bottom lip trembling as she attempted to prevent those tears from falling. 'I caught it on—'

'Don't even attempt to lie to me about this,' he advised softly. 'I assure you that you won't like me when I'm angry,' he added as he felt that red tide threatening to overwhelm and control him.

Samantha's eyes were wide, her throat moving convulsively as she swallowed. As clear evidence that she also saw and recognised that anger? That it frightened her?

Well, damn it, it frightened Xander too!

It was exactly what he had been running away from facing these past few weeks. The reason he had begun to avoid other people. The reason he had distanced himself from his family. And hadn't taken a woman to his bed. The very reason he had been so against Samantha and Daisy coming to live here with him in the first place.

Xander released Samantha abruptly before stepping away from her. 'Who hurt you, Samantha?' His gaze sharpened as a thought suddenly occurred to him. 'It was him, wasn't it? Your ex-husband,' he stated flatly. 'You saw him again this morning when you took Daisy to school. Did you *arrange* to meet him?'

'No! Absolutely not. Never,' Sam instantly denied the accusation, giving a shudder of distaste at the mere suggestion she would deliberately spend time with Malcolm ever again.

Except it was what she was thinking of doing

now, wasn't it? By giving in to Malcolm's demands?

She dropped down onto one of the stools at the breakfast bar. Before her knees buckled beneath her and she fell down.

'Samantha?'

'Just give me a minute or two.' She waved a hand dismissively in front of her face, head bent as she breathed in deeply.

'Do you still love him?'

Sam's gaze flew incredulously to the grimness of Xander's face. 'I absolutely do not!'

'Obviously.' Xander winced as he both heard and saw her obvious vehemence to the idea. 'So why would you—?' He paused, breathing softly. 'You were obviously upset after seeing him again on Saturday evening. He physically hurt you this morning, as well as upset you again. You're almost in tears now just talking about him.' He studied Sam intently. 'What hold does he have over you that you don't just tell him to go to—? Daisy.' Xander's brow cleared as realisation dawned. 'The bastard is threatening Daisy in some way.'

That red tide of anger rose even further at the thought of Samantha's ex-husband daring to threaten Daisey's happiness. In any way.

Bad enough that Samantha's ex-husband had physically hurt her today, the man deserved to be horse-whipped for that alone, but the thought that he might also have threatened Daisy in some way was totally unacceptable.

Xander came to a decision.

'Samantha.'

'Yes?' She raised her head to look up at him uncertainly.

'Samantha, I—' Xander drew in a deep breath, knowing he was about to take a huge leap of faith, but also knowing that he had no choice if he was to persuade Samantha into trusting him again.

He never talked about his abusive childhood to anyone, but if he wanted Samantha to talk to him now then he knew he had to tell her what had happened to him. That *he* now had to trust her, to confide in her, if he wanted her to trust and confide in him.

And he did want that. He wanted more than anything for Samantha to trust him.

He drew in a deep and ragged breath. 'Samantha, until I was twelve years old I lived with a father who enjoyed beating the hell out of me.'

She blinked, and then blinked again, as if she were having difficulty taking in what Xander had just told her. As no doubt she was. His childhood hardly fitted in with that charming billionaire playboy image the media were so fond of portraying.

An image that hid the vulnerability beneath.

A vulnerability Xander found himself surprisingly willing to share with Samantha.

'Darius, too?' she finally asked huskily.

A nerve pulsed in Xander's jaw. 'No, just me.'

Samantha moistened the dryness of her lips with the tip of her pink tongue. 'What happened when you were twelve?'

Xander's jaw tightened. 'My father died.'

Malcolm had been emotionally cruel, deliberately so, but he had never been physically violent, either towards herself or Daisy. Until today, Sam reminded herself with a frown.

Today Malcolm had felt absolutely no compunction about hurting her. In fact, she thought he had rather enjoyed it.

She swallowed. 'How?'

'Shortly after putting me in the hospital with a broken arm and concussion, my father fell down the stairs in a drunken stupor and broke his neck.'

'I don't recall any of this ever being in the newspapers.'

'It wasn't,' he confirmed abruptly. 'No one outside of my close family has ever known about the abuse.'

Sam was absolutely horrified at the thought of this man's childhood. 'Xander.'

'Samantha, I didn't tell you this so that your compassionate heart would feel sorry for me.'

'It doesn't,' she assured swiftly, knowing that Xander's pride was such that he wouldn't want, or welcome, pity from anyone. That the self-confident man he had become, the caring man *he* was towards Daisy, the empathy he had just shown her, were clear evidence that he had risen above his abusive childhood.

'Not even a little bit?'

'Well, of course a little bit!' Sam replied exasperatedly, a large part of her wishing that Xander's father were still alive, so that she could verbally upbraid him for his treatment of his son.

As a way of slaying Xander's dragon for him in a way that she couldn't seem to slay her own?

She grimaced. 'I would have to be completely heartless to remain immune to what you've just told me about your childhood,' she assured him briskly.

If he was honest with himself, Xander was feeling a little off-kilter now that he had actually spoken to Samantha about his father. He really didn't discuss his private life with people outside his family. Ever. And yet he had just done so with Samantha.

Admittedly it had been as a way of encouraging Samantha to feel that she could confide in him about her ex-husband, that she could trust him, but even so it was something Xander had never imagined sharing with any woman.

And yet…

He had confided in Samantha as a way of letting her know she could trust him with her own secrets, he had never imagined that by doing so he would somehow feel…free. As if a heavy weight had been lifted from his shoulders.

And his heart.

CHAPTER EIGHT

XANDER GAVE A humourless smile. 'Maybe you would feel differently about all that and about me, if I were to tell you that for the past few months I've been inwardly fighting the possibility that I might actually be like him?'

'That's utterly ridiculous,' Samantha dismissed without hesitation.

Xander's eyes widened at the absolute certainty in her voice. 'What makes you say that?'

She smiled confidently. 'I may not have known you for very long, Xander, but I do know you well enough to be able to see you are totally incapable of hurting a woman or a child. You obviously didn't want Daisy and I here, and yet you have been incredibly kind to both of us. So much so that Daisy adores you,' she added firmly even as she stepped forward to place the palm of her hand on Xander's chest.

'There's a good heart in there, Xander Sterne. A kind heart. One that wants to protect, not destroy.'

Xander looked down at her searchingly, breathing shallowly beneath the warm touch of her hand on his chest. 'Do you really believe that?' he finally asked.

'I know it.' Sam nodded.

Even after only a few days in his company Sam knew that initial fear she'd had, that he might be selfish and controlling like Malcolm, because he was even richer and more powerful than her ex-husband, wasn't even a possibility. Xander was arrogant and self-confident, and grumpy—no surprise given his present situation and the pain he was suffering.

But ultimately he had a good heart, a kind heart; his care and consideration of Daisy these past three days had proved that. As did his concern for her now. Sam had absolutely no doubt that Xander was a man who protected, that he was totally incapable of lashing out physically at a woman or child in temper.

'We may have our parents' genes, Xander,'

she said quietly. 'You have your father's, as Daisy has her father's, but I have yet to see any of Malcolm in Daisy. Or any of the father that you have just described to me in you.' Her eyed narrowed. 'You had your car accident six weeks ago?'

'Sorry?' Xander frowned at her sudden change of subject.

'You said that you've been questioning yourself for the past few months as to whether or not you might be like your father,' Sam reminded him as she stepped back and allowed her hand to fall back to her side. 'Did your accident have anything to do with that?'

Xander gave a rueful grimace at her astuteness. 'Something had been building inside me for weeks before that night, but that night I witnessed a man in the Midas nightclub verbally berating and humiliating the woman he was with. And I wanted to pulverise him into the ground,' he acknowledged grimly.

'A perfectly understandable reaction; *I* would have wanted to pulverise him too,' Samantha assured vehemently. 'Did you do it?'

'No.' A nerve pulsed in Xander's tightly clenched jaw. 'I wanted to, but somehow managed to keep control long enough to pass the problem off to security.'

'Doesn't that restraint prove to you that you're nothing like your father?' Samantha gave him an encouraging smile. 'That you never could be?'

Xander continued to look down at her for several long minutes, before drawing in a deep breath. 'Thank you for that. I appreciate it, after all I've just told you.'

He did appreciate Samantha's confidence, belief, in him. More than he could possibly say. More than he *dared* think about, when Samantha seemed so determined to keep him at arm's length, physically, at least. For the moment he would settle for her opening up to him emotionally.

'I want to help you, if I can, Samantha,' he encouraged gruffly. 'You aren't without powerful friends of your own now,' he pointed out softly. 'Andy and Darius. And now me.'

Was Xander her friend?

Sure, he had become fond of Daisy these past four days, but things had been so strained between the two of them since Saturday evening, that Sam had been sure Xander must be counting the days until she left his apartment.

His concern now and the confidences he had shared with her regarding his own childhood, while not exactly making them friends, had certainly broken down the barriers they had both been keeping about their emotions since Saturday evening.

'What did your ex-husband say to you this morning, Samantha?' he prompted gently.

She drew in a deep breath. 'Well, for one thing, he apparently isn't happy that Daisy and I are staying here in your apartment, even temporarily.'

'Tough.' Xander scowled. 'What else?'

'He wanted me to have dinner with him this evening.'

Xander stilled as he looked at Samantha.

'And are you going to accept the invitation?'

'I already turned him down.' She gave a

humourless smile. 'And it was more of a threat than an invitation.'

'What does he want besides dinner?' Xander rasped harshly. As if he couldn't guess. As if he didn't already *know* what the man wanted!

Samantha was an incredibly beautiful woman, a woman with a warm and loving heart; any man would have to be completely stupid to have ever let her go in the first place.

'He wants me to become his mistress,' Samantha confirmed, her gaze no longer able to meet his.

Xander drew in a deep controlling breath, continuing to breathe deeply until he felt capable of talking again. 'And how does he intend to retaliate if you don't agree to that?'

The colour drained from Sam's cheeks. 'He said he'll apply to the court for visiting rights with Daisy. Which I can't allow to happen,' she continued emotionally. 'Malcolm never wanted Daisy in the first place. He ignored her very existence when we lived with him, by imposing all sorts of ridiculous rules regarding her behaviour. And he's had absolutely no interest in seeing her since the two of us parted and divorced.'

A nerve pulsed in Xander's tightly clenched jaw at the thought of any man—any father!—ignoring his own daughter in that way.

Although it certainly explained why it was Daisy never visited her father and why Samantha didn't want her to now.

It also explained the way Samantha had bristled with reaction to that list of rules Xander had come out with the evening she and Daisy arrived here.

No way, absolutely no way, was Xander going to allow Samantha's ex-husband to bully and blackmail her into doing what he wanted. Into forcing her to share his bed.

'Exactly who is he, Samantha?' he grated. 'Well you've already told me his name isn't Smith,' he rasped as Samantha looked up at him questioningly.

'Howard.' She swallowed, her gaze now avoiding meeting his. 'His name is Malcolm Howard.'

Xander's eyes narrowed. 'Of Howard Electronics? *That* Malcolm Howard?' He only knew the other man by reputation, mostly to do with business, although he seemed to recall hearing Howard had been married briefly a few years ago. He didn't remember ever hearing mention of a child from that marriage, though. Obviously that was because Howard had chosen never to tell anyone about the daughter he had no interest in.

Samantha drew in a deep breath. 'You know him?'

Xander shook his head. 'Not personally. I seem to recall he has a membership to the Midas nightclub.' A privilege Xander was now going to look into cancelling at the earliest opportunity! 'Darius knows him far better than I do. Of course, that's what Howard was doing at the hotel on Saturday; he was one of the evening guests invited to Darius and Miranda's wedding.'

'Yes.'

'I'm pretty sure Darius has no idea what sort of man he is.' Xander scowled. 'Did you know he—? No,' he answered his own question impatiently. 'You had absolutely no idea your ex-husband was going to be at the wedding too. If you had you would have made sure to leave before he arrived. Or possibly you would not have gone to the wedding at all.'

'No.'

'What did he do to you when you were married to him, Samantha?' Xander pressed softly.

She looked up at him wordlessly for several long seconds, a frown creasing her creamy brow. And then that frown cleared as she glanced down at her bandaged wrist. 'Emotional cruelty can be just as unpleasant as physical violence.'

He knew that, had watched his father torment and control his mother and brother for years, by physically threatening Xander. Just as Malcolm Howard's threats now, regarding Daisy, were designed to deliberately torment Samantha, to control her.

To a point that she was actually thinking of giving in to Howard's demands?

Over Xander's dead body was that going to happen.

He gave a shake of his head.

'Malcolm Howard is a very wealthy man, and yet you and Daisy—' He hesitated, wincing his discomfort as he realised what he had been about to say.

'And yet Daisy and I live in a one-bedroomed flat and I work at jobs like this one, and the one at Andy's studio, to make ends meet.' Samantha obviously felt no such reticence.

'Yes.' He frowned darkly.

She gave a rueful grimace. 'You already know so much, so why shouldn't you know the rest? Malcolm offered me a deal when I divorced him, a small monthly maintenance payment for Daisy, no alimony or settlement for me, the return of all the jewellery and gifts he had given me during our marriage, and in exchange he would give me full custody of Daisy.'

'Full custody of the child he didn't want in the first place?' Xander said softly.

'Yes.' She smiled shakily.

Xander had never heard of anything so diabolical in his life. It was utterly disgusting. Malcolm Howard was worth millions, and yet he had begrudged his ex-wife even the small amount of money she needed to be able to take care of her daughter?

A diabolical deal he was now threatening to renege on unless Samantha gave in to his demand that she become his mistress.

What sort of man did that to the woman he had once been married to, the same woman who was the mother of his child?

'Do you trust me, Samantha?' Xander asked huskily.

'To do what?' She eyed him warily.

'To help you and Daisy?'

To make sure that Howard suffered, in the way he had made Samantha and Daisy suffer, in the past, and now!

Did Sam trust Xander? It had been so long since she had relied on anyone. Since she had *trusted* anyone enough to rely on them; she had thought she could trust and rely on Malcolm once, and look how well that had turned out!

'Don't think about the past for now, Samantha,' Xander encouraged as he obviously saw, and guessed, the reason for her frown. 'Just concentrate on whether or not you trust me to find a way that will free you, and Daisy, of your ex-husband's hold on you once and for all.'

Did she want Xander to do that? Was this the answer, the miracle, she had been praying for earlier?

Did Sam really have any choice but to trust Xander, when her own and Daisy's future hung so precariously in the balance, once again because of Malcolm's threats?

She moistened the dryness of her lips before speaking. 'Why would you even want to help us? It isn't your problem.'

'I'm making it so,' he insisted grimly.

Sam looked at him wonderingly. 'You really are a sheep in wolf's clothing, aren't you?'

His mouth twisted wryly at that description. 'I'm actually a wolf in a wolf's clothing. But even wolves have a heart, Samantha. And, for obvious reasons, I utterly despise bullies,' he added harshly. 'So...' he straightened '...will you let me help you?'

Sam looked at him for several long seconds

before she slowly nodded her head. 'He gave me until the end of the week to make my decision.'

'Big of him.'

'He seemed to think so, yes.'

'I'll have something in place by then,' Xander assured her grimly.

'Then, yes,' she accepted huskily. 'Yes, I'll gladly let you help me, if you really want to.'

'I want to.' He nodded tersely.

Sam lived in a state of trepidation for the next four days. Malcolm had given her until the end of the week to make her decision, but she knew him too well to believe anything he said, and lived in fear of him waiting for her at Daisy's school again one morning or evening.

And she worried even more when the days passed and she heard nothing further from him.

Xander had assured her he had the situation under control, when Sam had voiced her concerns a couple of days before, adding that he would have some positive news for her by the end of the week.

But he must also have been concerned Malcolm might turn up again at Daisy's school because he had insisted on accompanying them in the car to and from school these past four mornings. Much to Daisy's delight.

And so giving Sam another worry—that her daughter was becoming altogether too attached to Xander. They all ate their meals together now, and had done since Sunday morning when Xander had insisted he would be eating all of his meals in the kitchen in future. And it was Xander who Daisy was eager to see when she came out of school every day. Xander that Daisy asked to read her a story every night before she went to sleep.

Which was exactly what he was doing on Friday evening while Sam cleared away in the kitchen after dinner.

It was all a bit too cosy for comfort.

Sam's comfort, at least; Xander and Daisy seemed perfectly happy with the arrangement.

So, along with worrying about Malcolm, she also had the extra worry of how Daisy was going to react when the two of them had to move out of Xander's apartment in just over a week's time.

Not that Sam didn't completely understand Daisy's infatuation; she was afraid she had one of those going herself where Xander was concerned.

As if by tacit agreement, the two of them hadn't spoken again of the things Xander had told her of his childhood. But the knowledge of those shared confidences was there between them, nonetheless, creating a subtle but discernible shift in their relationship. There was an unspoken companionship between them now, coupled with that underlying physical awareness. The latter on Sam's part, at least.

Xander had made no attempt to step over the line with Sam again, and that was despite the fact that his desire was more than obvious every time she helped him in and out of the shower!

And was that disappointment she was feeling?

Because Xander hadn't made a single attempt to kiss her again?

Was she actually feeling a little *jealous* of the closeness that existed between Xander and Daisy?

No, not jealous exactly; how could Sam possibly resent any kindness and affection Xander might show towards Daisy? It was just that she ached to be closer to him herself.

'Everything okay?'

She almost dropped the plate she was placing in the dishwasher at Xander's unexpected reappearance in the kitchen. Usually she was able to hear his progress down the hallway on his crutches, but the daily physio sessions were going so well that the physiotherapist had advised just yesterday that he need only use the walking stick now. After which Sam had been caught out more than once when Xander appeared unexpectedly in a room.

She placed the plate in the dishwasher before straightening, her gaze focused somewhere over Xander's left shoulder as he stood in the doorway; she was far too physically aware of him after her recent thoughts. 'I was just wondering what Daisy and I should do over the weekend.'

Xander stepped fully into the room, immediately dwarfing what had previously seemed a spacious room. 'Strange, the two of us were just discussing that too. Daisy would like us to take her to the cinema tomorrow and then she suggested we all go swimming.'

Sam's heart sank at the thought of a Xander-filled weekend; hours and hours when she would have to hide the growing feelings she had for him. 'I really appreciate all the time and effort you've taken with Daisy this past week—' she began.

'But?' He quirked one blond brow.

Sam still couldn't look at him directly, that disturbing awareness of him thrumming beneath her skin. 'But perhaps you shouldn't spend quite as much time with her as you do? Daisy shouldn't come to rely on your attention so much,' she added regretfully. 'We're going to be leaving here at the end of next week, and—'

'And you think I'm then just going to forget

all about her, is that it?' Xander barked harshly, more than a little insulted by that assumption. 'You said you trusted me, Samantha,' he said gruffly.

'I *do* trust you.' Samantha chewed on her bottom lip. 'It's just—I appreciate the time you've spent with Daisy, I really do. It's simply that I know you're still incapacitated, at the moment, and can't do the things you usually do,' she hurried on as Xander scowled. 'That it must be boring for you being stuck in this apartment all the time, as well as frustrating. But you're improving rapidly, and once you're completely fit again, you'll obviously want to return to your own life, and—'

'And then I'll no longer have time for Daisy, is that what you're saying?' Xander realised that he and Samantha had deliberately not discussed personal subjects again since revealing so much about themselves to each other on Monday. Possibly because neither of them were used to doing that? But Samantha's implication now, that he was just going to cast Daisy aside like a pair of old shoes once he was fit again, was hardly fair.

He had grown genuinely fond of Daisy. For herself. But also, Xander knew, because she was a miniature version of her mother.

He had grown more than a little fond of Samantha too. In fact, the desire he felt to make love to her was now a physical ache that he lived with on a daily basis. A desire he was determinedly denying himself from even attempting to satisfy, because he knew he shouldn't take advantage of this situation.

Maybe it was selfish of him, but he had been putting off discussing Howard with Samantha again, had enjoyed this past week too much, having Samantha relax in his company, having her trust him, to want to ruin that peace and harmony. He had even taken to having cold showers every morning, in an effort not to ruin that trust by attempting to kiss her again!

That Samantha should now more or less accuse him of using Daisy as a diversion for his *boredom,* and that he would forget about her, and Samantha, once he was fit enough to resume his own life, just added salt to the wound.

Did those confidences he had shared with her about his father mean nothing to her? And what of the trust she had placed in him by agreeing to let him help her?

'Well, thanks for that, Samantha,' he grated. 'Nice to know you think me insensitive as well as shallow!' He turned abruptly, leaving the kitchen to walk down the hallway, and shut himself in his study before sitting down heavily behind his desk.

Before he said anything he might regret.

Such as, that he hadn't been bored for a single moment these last few days.

That, despite the initial doubts he had voiced to Darius on the subject he *liked* having Samantha and Daisy living with him, and genuinely enjoyed their company.

That he woke up every morning with a smile on his face, in anticipation of spending the day with them.

That he had the feeling his apartment was

going to have all the warmth of a morgue after they left next weekend.

That it was testament to how *much* he liked Samantha that he had shared those confidences of his childhood, a subject he had never discussed with anyone outside his immediate family.

Damn it, Xander valued all of those things so highly that he had deliberately chosen to keep his desire for Samantha to himself, for fear that it might damage the peaceful existence they now had.

Maybe he did need to get out of his apartment for a while, away from both Samantha and Daisy, and try to get some perspective back into his life?

His assistant had been arriving promptly at the apartment at nine-thirty every morning this week so that the two of them could spend an hour or so going through what needed to be dealt with urgently, and what could wait until Darius either came back from his honeymoon or Xander was fit enough to spend the day in his office.

But he hadn't been out of his apartment for weeks on a social basis, apart from to attend the wedding last weekend.

Security was downstairs, so Samantha would be safe enough from her ex-husband in his apartment, and a couple of hours checking out the Midas nightclub might be just what Xander needed to put himself, and this situation, back into perspective.

'Xander?'

He had been so lost in deep and brooding thought that he hadn't even heard Samantha open the study door. She hovered in the doorway looking across at him uncertainly.

She looked so very beautiful, with her flame-coloured hair loose and curling about her shoulders and down her back, her face slightly flushed from cooking and clearing away after dinner. Her small and perfectly rounded breasts were pert against the white fitted shirt she wore, her tailored black trousers clinging lovingly to the sweet curve of her hips and bottom.

Xander's body reacted sharply to the sight of her.

So much so that the need he now felt, to stand up and move restlessly about his study, became an impossibility. 'What is it, Samantha?' he enquired softly.

'I wanted to apologise. I didn't mean to imply—I know that you genuinely care for Daisy—I just don't want—I would never deliberately insult you,' she finished lamely.

'Just indirectly,' Xander drawled. 'Let's just forget it,' he dismissed. 'You were probably right to be concerned.' He shrugged. 'I am basically shallow and insensitive.'

'I didn't say that.'

'No, I did.' He sighed. 'What do I know about five-year-olds anyway?'

'Well, you were once one yourself.'

Yes, he had been, and he knew exactly how it had felt to be so young and so totally bewildered by his own father's dislike of him. As Malcolm Howard's years of lack of interest in his own daughter seemed to imply the other man also disliked Daisy.

So yes, on that level Xander could relate totally to Daisy.

It was the increasing desire he felt to make love to her mother that had become the biggest danger.

'Let's not argue, Xander.' Tears glistened in her eyes as Samantha looked across at him imploringly. 'This business with Malcolm has unsettled me. I certainly didn't mean to insult you by anything I said earlier.'

Xander knew that. Knew that Samantha wasn't the type of woman to ever deliberately insult or hurt anyone. She was sweet and kind, and had been infinitely patient and understanding from the onset, despite his bad-temperedness. She was also a wonderful mother to Daisy.

Nor did he have a single regret about telling her about his own childhood; he knew that it had been necessary at the time. It had also, in some strange inexplicable way, continued to act as a balm to his own feelings about the past.

He drew in a deep and ragged breath. 'You're obviously tense and worried about your ex, and I should probably have talked to you about this sooner.' He sighed heavily. 'I didn't because…' He paused, knowing it had been selfish of him to want to keep the status quo for as long as possible. 'After making extensive enquiries about Malcolm Howard, I've decided to make my strike against him through his business,' he revealed grimly. 'In fact, I've already set those plans in motion. Don't look so worried.' He gave Samantha a reassuring smile. 'By the time I've finished with him Howard will wish he had never so much as spoken to you again, let alone threatened you by using Daisy.'

She gave a worried frown. 'What are you going to do?'

'What *am* I doing?' Xander corrected grimly as he stood up, his erection having finally subsided. 'Howard Electronics is shortly going to experience a severe problem with the loan they're currently requesting from their bank, putting in jeopardy the plans Howard currently has for expansion into the Japanese market,' he added with satisfaction.

Xander had also cancelled Howard's membership to the Midas nightclub the day after he and Samantha had spoken, a move guaranteed to ensure the other man knew exactly where his troubles were coming from. It shouldn't take too long, once Howard discovered his membership to Midas had been discontinued, for the other man to make enquiries and realise Xander was also behind the difficulty with his bank loan. A deliberate move on Xander's part, to ensure that he became Howard's target, rather than Samantha or Daisy.

'You can do that?' Samantha eyed him doubtfully.

Xander gave a grim smile of satisfaction. 'I can when it turns out I have a financial interest in the bank Howard uses. At the moment he is running around like a headless chicken trying to secure a loan from another bank.'

'And what happens when he stops running around in circles?' She frowned.

Xander grimaced. 'My lawyer will have contacted him before then, strongly suggesting Howard comes to his office for a meeting. A meeting at which, in exchange for a guaranteed loan from me, with a low interest rate, he will sign a contract agreeing never to come near you or Daisy ever again. This needs to be settled once and for all, Samantha,' he insisted huskily as he saw she still looked worried.

'What if he still doesn't agree?'

'He will.' Because if he didn't Xander would feel no compunction whatsoever in breaking the other man completely.

She gave a shake of her head. 'I can't let you do that.'

'It's already done, Samantha.'

Sam could only stare at him. This was insane. Unbelievable. She had known Xander was extremely rich, but it seemed he was even more powerful than she could ever have imagined. And she had never dreamt that he would go to such lengths on her own and Daisy's behalf.

Xander took a step forward to look down at her searchingly. 'I won't let him hurt you, or Daisy, again, Samantha.'

That was laudable, it really was, except that Sam had realised these past few days that it was Xander himself who was now capable of hurting her, far more than Malcolm ever had, but in a completely different way.

She had been fighting her attraction to him

all week, avoiding being alone with him whenever possible, as well as keeping their conversations light and impersonal. It hadn't always been possible to remain completely immune, of course; shower time with Xander had become both Sam's daily torture and pleasure. Especially given his blatant desire.

But Sam had put his arousal down to the weeks he had been denied a sex life, rather than a direct response to her. Xander was probably so sexually frustrated, after almost two months of drought, that he would have responded physically to any woman, rather than specifically to her.

Nevertheless, that hadn't prevented Sam's own reaction to all that taut, tanned, and naked flesh: wide and muscled shoulders she ached to touch, a sleek and lean chest, his waist and hips narrow, his legs long and muscled.

His hair had also grown longer this past week, falling in shaggy blond waves onto the back of the rounded neckline of his T-shirts, and falling silkily over his forehead.

He looked even more like a sleek and muscled Viking about to plunder and pillage and—

'Samantha?' Xander queried huskily as he took in the slightly fevered glow to her eyes and the delicate flush that had appeared in her cheeks, the tenseness of silence between them now such that he could hear the clock ticking out in the hallway.

Her gaze was focused on his mouth as she moistened the plumpness of her own recently chewed lips with a sweep of her tongue. 'I should get back to the kitchen.'

'I thought you had finished in there for the night?'

She looked flustered. 'I— Not quite. I—I'll leave you to—to get on with whatever it was you were doing when I interrupted you.'

He shrugged. 'I was just sitting here thinking of going out.'

She raised startled eyes. 'You were?'

'To the club.' Xander nodded. 'But I'd really rather stay here. With you.'

Dark lashes fanned against Samantha's cheeks as she lowered her lids. 'You would?'

'Look at me, Samantha.'

She gave a slow shake of her head. 'I'd really rather not.'

'Why not?'

Her gaze flickered up to his and then quickly away again.

Clearly she had seen and correctly read the desire he was no longer making any effort to hide.

The same desire he had been fighting for the past week. A desire he wasn't sure he was capable of fighting any longer. He wanted Samantha so much right now he could no longer think straight. And her scent was driving him insane; insidiously warm and desirable woman combined with an underlying floral smell, possibly lavender soap?

'This really is a bad idea, Xander.'

'The most enjoyable ones usually are.' He stepped forward to take her in his arms, the softness of her curves instantly accommodating his much harder ones.

She placed her hands on his shoulders in an effort to hold her body away from him. 'We really shouldn't do this, Xander.' Her voice was pleading, asking for a level-headedness he simply couldn't give her right now.

'Do you really want me to stop?' Xander murmured throatily.

Of course Sam didn't want him to stop, not when his lips and tongue were tasting the dips and hollows of her throat, his teeth gently biting her earlobe, his breath warm against her skin.

'We could always look on it as research,' he murmured throatily, his hands roaming the length of her spine as his lips now plundered the sensitive hollows at the base of her throat, the five o'clock shadow on his chin a pleasurable rasp against her sensitive flesh. 'A way of settling once and for all which position is most comfortable for me to make love?' he teasingly reminded her of that previous conversation.

Sam knew that she really shouldn't let this go any further than it already had. But it had been so long since a man had touched her in this way. Since any man had touched her with such gentle appreciation. As it had the week before, her long-denied body betrayed her, reacting instinctively to just the thought of that pleasure, her breasts swelling, nipples hardening to sensitive pebbles, and heat building between her thighs.

Xander smelled so good too, a light and spicy cologne, and the lemon shampoo she knew he used to wash his hair. There was an underlying smell that was all Xander; a healthy male in his sexual prime.

Sam *wanted* this.

Wanted Xander.

Surely any regrets could come later?

And she had no doubt there would be regrets. The main one being that she could never mean anything more to Xander than a single night— or possibly two, if she was lucky!—of pleasure.

But other women went to bed with men all the time just for the pleasure of it, so why not her?

Yes, why the hell not her?

Xander didn't need to profess undying love for her to be a caring and considerate lover. A lover she already knew was capable of giving her pleasure. Any more than she needed to be in love with him in order to give him that same pleasure.

Live a little, Sam, she mentally encouraged herself. *Take what he is offering and think of the consequences later.*

She looked up at him sharply. 'I'm not on any sort of contraception.' She couldn't think of *those* consequences later.

His eyes darkened at the realisation her comment signalled her capitulation. 'I'll take care of it,' he assured her gruffly.

Of course he would; no doubt Xander had a bedside drawer full of condoms. After all, who knew when he was going to get lucky?

Could she really do this? Indulge in hot and meaningless sex with a man—with Xander— just for the pleasure of it?

Oh, yes!

CHAPTER NINE

SHE LOOKED UP at Xander shyly. 'Your bedroom or mine?'

Xander gave her an approving smile as he released her before taking her hand firmly in his much larger one. 'My bedroom is where the condoms are,' he reminded teasingly as they walked out of the study together and down the silence of the hallway.

Sam felt her cheeks warm at the intimacy of their conversation. Which was pretty silly of her, when she intended getting naked with this man in just a few minutes' time.

Xander turned on a softly glowing bedside lamp as they entered the masculine bedroom, dominated by the opulence of the four-poster bed. That beautiful mahogany bed was covered with an abundance of gold and cream silk pillows and bedcover, and had matching drapes tied back at the four sides and the two windows.

Decadence personified.

As was the beautiful Viking god at her side.

'Stop over-thinking, Samantha,' Xander encouraged gruffly as he saw the uncertainty in Samantha's expression as she looked at the bed, and easily guessed the reason for it; she had already revealed that he would be her first lover since her husband. 'It's going to be fine, trust me,' he encouraged softly even as he ran the soft pad of his thumb over the enticing pout of her bottom lip.

'I just—I don't want to disappoint you.'

'I don't want to disappoint you either.'

'You couldn't!'

'Lovemaking is all about learning what pleases the other person, giving as well as receiving,' Xander reassured her gruffly. 'And I do want to give to you, Samantha,' he added huskily. 'Feel how much I want you.' He placed one of her hands over his jeans, against his arousal.

Xander watched in fevered fascination as

Samantha moistened the fullness of her lips with the tip of her tongue.

In anticipation of running that moist tongue over the throbbing fullness she cupped in her hand?

Xander certainly hoped so.

He held her gaze as he took her with him and moved back slightly until he was able to sit on the side of the bed and stand her in between his parted thighs. His gaze continued to hold the shyness of hers captive as he began to unfasten the buttons of the fitted white shirt she was wearing.

His breath caught in his throat as he slid the unfastened shirt down her arms to reveal the white satin and lace bra she wore beneath, the paleness of her skin a pearly white. 'You're so beautiful,' he groaned in appreciation as his fingers caressed lightly across the swell of her breasts and down the length of her slender waist. 'So, so beautiful, Samantha,' he murmured, his arms about her waist as he nuzzled his face against the heated softness of her breasts encased in satin and lace.

Sam could barely breathe as she rested her hands on Xander's shoulders for balance, the intimacy of this situation so beautiful. Utterly, utterly beautiful.

As was the man now kissing the tops of her breasts, his lips a heated caress as his hands roamed restlessly along the slender length of her back.

His hair felt soft beneath the fingers she entwined in its silky length, his T-shirt an arousing abrasion against her bared flesh as he continued to nuzzle and kiss her breasts.

Xander moved back slightly. 'This has to come off,' he murmured achingly even as his fingers dealt deftly with the fastening at the back of her bra and he slipped the straps down and off her arms before dropping it onto the carpet with her shirt. His eyes darkened to black as he drank in the sight of her naked breasts. 'I absolutely love this.' His fingers stroked lightly across the soaring eagle tattoo. 'It's almost as beautiful as you are.'

Sam *felt* beautiful under Xander's appreciative ministrations, her breath catching in her throat as she felt the first touch of his lips against a bared nipple. Gently kissing first one, and then the other, over and over again, his tongue a slow and velvety rasp against her engorged flesh.

She made a husky groan of need in her throat, wanting, needing.

'Yes!' she hissed weakly, her fingers tightening in Xander's hair and holding him to her as he finally suckled one ripe and aching berry deep into the heat of his mouth, his tongue no longer velvety as it rasped over and against that arousal at the same time as his hand cupped her other breast, rolling her nipple between finger and thumb.

Sam's back arched into those caresses as the pleasure gathered between the heat of her thighs as she moved restlessly against him.

Xander fell back against the silk pillows covering the bed, taking Samantha with him, so that she now lay above him, her parted legs straddling his thighs.

He lay his head back on the pillows, lids narrowed as he cupped her beautiful and responsive breasts. Petite and firm, they were perfectly rounded, with deep rose-coloured nipples that were just begging for more attention from his hands and mouth.

Xander pushed the aching in his left thigh to the back of his mind as he raised his head slightly, his gaze deliberately holding hers as he slowly laved one ripe and juicy nipple with his tongue before suckling her deeply into the heat of his mouth, groaning low in his throat, his own arousal pulsing against her heat. He saw Samantha close her eyes in pleasure, an aroused flush to her cheeks as she leant into him, allowing him to suckle her deeper as she rested her hands on the pillows beside his head.

Sam looked down at Xander as she told herself over and over again in her head that she could do this, that she could just enjoy the moment. Enjoy Xander.

She gasped as his mouth on her breasts took her to a level of pleasure she had never experienced before, her position above him allowing her to arch herself slowly and rhythmically against him, the hardness of his arousal pressing against the heat between her thighs, the two layers of denim between them acting as an extra abrasion, until her breath came in short pleasurable gasps and she knew herself to be teetering on the edge of climax.

As if aware of that, Xander bit down onto her aching nipple at the same time as the finger and thumb of his other hand squeezed its twin, sending Sam over the edge of that pleasure and into the most intense and pleasurably prolonged orgasm of her life.

Sam gasped again as she rode out the pleasure of that orgasm, until her arms gave way and she collapsed against Xander's rapidly rising and falling chest, his breath a harsh rasp against her as his arms wrapped around her.

She lay weakly against him, her own breathing ragged as her body pulsed in the aftershocks of that pleasure.

'Are you okay, Samantha?' Xander finally asked.

Was she okay? Sam had never felt so okay before in her life.

She felt liberated. She had experienced a freedom she had never known before.

Before Xander.

Her gaze was sultry as she sat up and looked down at him, feeling a triumphant thrill as she saw his eyes were dark with his own arousal; there was a flush to his cheeks, the gold of his hair tousled from the caress of her fingers.

'I think we found the comfortable position, don't you?' Sam teased huskily as she continued to hold his gaze as she slid slowly down the length of his body, kneeling between his parted thighs as her fingers moved to the fastening at the front of his jeans.

She felt emboldened as Xander looked at her between narrowed lids, as she slipped the three buttons loose, revealing that he wore black body-hugging boxers beneath, his desire long and thick. Sam scooted back to pull his jeans down the long length of his muscled legs before discarding them completely.

She unfastened and pushed off her own trousers and panties before running her hands along the length of his long and muscled legs, from ankle to thigh, pausing to caress the slightly reddened scar on his left thigh, before her hands moved higher still, lightly caressing the length of his arousal through the thin material of his briefs.

'Take them off, Samantha!' Xander groaned as he moved restlessly against her, hands clenched into fists at his sides. 'I want to feel your hands against me.'

He was just so gorgeous, Sam groaned inwardly as she slowly lowered the boxers, hardly aware of discarding them as her heated gaze remained fixed on the long and throbbing length of his arousal.

'Touch me, Samantha,' Xander encouraged gruffly. 'Yes, just like that!' He groaned achingly, his eyes closing as she curled the fingers of her hand about him and lowered her head to take him into the heat of her mouth.

Xander felt his control slipping within minutes as he watched Samantha's head slowly bob up and down, the fullness of her lips wide about him, her wicked tongue rasping the length of him, the tingling at the base of his spine tell-ing him he was very close to release.

His hands were gentle on her shoulders as he pulled her up and away from him, knowing he had to stop the torment before he did just that. 'Not like that, Samantha,' he groaned as he saw the disappointment of her expression. 'I want to be inside you,' he explained as he reached over and opened the top drawer of the bedside cabinet before taking out a condom.

'Let me,' Samantha offered huskily as she took the packet from him, tearing off the top before taking it out.

Xander felt that renewed tingling at the base of his spine as Samantha's caressing fingers slowly rolled it over and then down the length of him, fearing that he wasn't going to last long once he was buried to the hilt inside her heat. Not sure he was even going to last that long if he didn't get inside her right now.

'On top of me,' he grated. 'I need to be in-side you now,' he encouraged gruffly, his hands on her hips as he entered her, trying to take it slowly.

Knowing he had lost the battle the moment he was fully buried inside Samantha. 'I can't! Forgive me, Samantha, but I just can't take this slowly. Next time. I promise next time,' he groaned achingly as he held onto her hips as he began to thrust into her.

Sam tightly gripped his shoulders as she rode the fierceness of his lengthy thrusts, her body flooding with desire as she revelled in the intensity of need she could see in Xander's almost pained expression, his fingers digging into her hips as he pushed hard and deep.

Her eyes widened in shock as she felt a second climax building rapidly inside her. 'Xander!' she had time to cry before that climax crested, and then broke with an intensity of pleasure even stronger than the first.

As if that was all he had been waiting for, Xander cried out at his own release thrusting hard and deep as he pulsed hotly inside her.

What a fool she had been, Sam acknowledged regretfully the following morning as she looked down at the beautiful man sleeping in the bed beside her, knowing there could be no next time for the two of them.

Because no matter what she might have told herself last night when the two of them made love, the reassurance she had given herself to believe she could have casual sex with a man, with Xander, before just as happily walking away, was all nonsense. A lie she had told herself because she had wanted, desired, Xander so very much.

Now she realised not only had she lied to herself about the casual sex, but also about her feelings for Xander.

And those regrets that could come later?

Well, they had come crashing down about her head the moment Sam had been woken at five o'clock this morning, the sun streaming in through the window of his bedroom, because they had forgotten to draw the curtains the evening before.

Sam had felt totally disorientated when she'd first woken up, taking several seconds to get her bearings, before remembering exactly where she was, and then turning sharply to look down at the man sleeping in the bed beside her.

One look at Xander's beautifully chiselled face relaxed in sleep, and that gloriously tousled blond hair fanned out on the pillow behind him, with only a thin sheet covering the nakedness of his hips and thighs, leaving his muscled chest bare, and Sam had realised she was in love with him.

That somewhere, somehow, during this past week of sharing an apartment with him—of sharing her past with him; of him sharing the horrors of his childhood with her, and the battle he had suffered these past few weeks, fearing he might be like his father; of just *being* with Xander constantly; of feeling moved by his protectiveness towards her and his kindness to Daisy—Sam had fallen deeply in love with him.

Which was why she was now going to climb quietly and carefully out of his bed, taking care not to disturb or wake him, and go back to her own bedroom.

To consider how she was ever going to face Xander again.

At least she didn't have to make the walk of shame, and could simply gather up her scattered clothes from the bedroom floor and walk the short way down the hallway in order to reach the relative sanctuary of her bedroom.

No doubt there had been dozens of women between Xander's bed sheets over the years. Beautiful women. Sophisticated women. Those same beautiful and sophisticated women who could enjoy casual sex with as accomplished a lover as Xander Sterne, before dressing the following morning and walking away without any regrets.

Unfortunately, Sam now knew she wasn't *any* of those things.

She wasn't beautiful, or sophisticated, but worst of all she certainly wasn't capable of walking away from Xander without regrets.

Any more than she had wanted to see Xander's disappointment if he should wake up and feel regret at finding her there beside him in his bed.

* * *

Xander felt wonderfully relaxed when he woke up, the warmth of the morning sun shining across his face and closed lids.

Thoroughly relaxed. And wonderfully satiated in a way he could never remember feeling before. Almost as if he— Not almost. He *had* made love with Samantha.

Xander's eyes opened wide and he turned sharply to look at the bed beside him, the events of the previous night washing over him in bright and glorious colour.

He sat up abruptly as he saw the bed beside him was empty. As was his bedroom, Samantha's clothes gone from the carpeted floor. Nor could he hear any sounds coming from the adjoining bathroom, as evidence that Samantha was taking a shower.

The clock on the bedside table read only six o'clock, so where was she?

Gone, came his immediate answer.

Just to her own bedroom, or from his apartment completely?

Even if Samantha regretted what had happened between the two of them—and her disappearing act seemed to imply she did—surely she wouldn't have woken Daisy up in the middle of the night and just left without saying a word to him? Especially with her ex-husband on the prowl and ready to pounce.

No, Xander was sure Samantha wouldn't have done that.

But there was no denying she *had* left his bedroom.

Why?

She'd seemed happy enough the night before, as she had snuggled comfortably in his arms before they both fell into an exhausted sleep.

Damn it. He had been so thoroughly satiated the previous night, so exhausted by their lovemaking after suffering weeks of physical limitations, that he hadn't even woken when Samantha crept from his bed!

He now ran an agitated hand through his already tousled hair, the tenderness of his scalp reminding him of the way she had tightly gripped his hair when she climaxed a second time as he'd fiercely thrust and pulsed inside her.

Now she had gone, crept from his bed like a thief in the night. As if last night had meant nothing to her. As if *he* meant nothing to her.

And perhaps he didn't, Xander realised with a frown, as he recalled their conversation just before they had made love. Their discussion of the problem of her ex-husband, and the way in which he intended dealing with that problem, for both her own and Daisy's sakes.

Could Samantha have gone to bed with him, made love, out of *gratitude* for just the thought of that help reaching fruition?

Because he had made it obvious he wanted her, and she hadn't liked to say no?

'Cereal, pancakes, or eggs and bacon?' Sam prompted briskly as Xander made an appearance in the kitchen doorway just after eight o'clock, her daughter already seated at the breakfast bar eating the last of her pancakes.

It was a grim-faced Xander who looked at her with dark and wary eyes, nothing like the wild and satisfying lover of the night before. Or the relaxed and satiated man Sam had left asleep in bed earlier this morning.

Any more than she looked—or felt—like the uninhibited woman of the night before.

Her cheeks felt warm just thinking of the intimacies the two of them had shared the previous night. 'Or maybe just your usual coffee?' she carried on hurriedly as Xander made no reply but just continued to look at her searchingly with those dark and enigmatic eyes.

But searching for what?

Regrets?

Sam had plenty of those!

Rebuke?

She had absolutely nothing to rebuke Xander for, had been a more than willing participant to their lovemaking.

So what was Xander looking for as he gazed at her so intently?

Whatever it was, he didn't seem to have found it, the expression in his dark eyes becoming even more guarded as he stepped further into the kitchen. 'Just coffee is fine, thanks,' he answered as he moved to sit opposite Daisy. 'How are you this morning, Daisy-flower?' His voice noticeably softened as he spoke to the little girl.

Sam efficiently poured coffee into a mug and placed it in front of him before collecting up Daisy's empty plate and returning to tidy up the stove top, her back turned towards the room as tears blurred her vision.

This was awful. Worse than she had even imagined it might be.

In her imaginings there had at least been a stilted conversation between herself and Xander, in which he would say something like *you were right, last night was a bad idea*, and Sam would urge him to forget about it, as she already had.

The fact that Daisy was present this morning, and would be all weekend, was going to make even that brief conversation difficult, if not impossible.

And Sam wasn't sure her already frayed nerves could take the added tension, especially if Xander decided to spend time with them this weekend.

Because they weren't a normal family. And they never could be.

Xander's past record, of having been involved with a legion of women, clearly spoke for itself, and he certainly hadn't made any rash declarations of love to Sam the evening before. He hadn't needed to, she reminded herself, after she had made it more than obvious she'd wanted him as much as he'd wanted her.

She had been a willing scratch to Xander's itch, at best. And the fact that he meant so much more to her than that wasn't his problem.

That was something Sam definitely intended keeping to herself.

Xander would run a mile if he thought for one moment that she had feelings for him. Worse, that she had been stupid enough to fall in love with him.

Just the thought of leaving Xander at the end of next week, of never seeing him again, was enough to break her heart.

'Daisy, how about I put a cartoon on for you?' Xander suggested lightly as he stood up, very aware of the fact that Samantha was keeping her back turned towards the two of them for a reason; the slight shaking of her shoulders, and the occasional soft sniff he could hear, clearly indicating that she was crying.

Could he feel any more of a heel than he already did? Xander wondered heavily as he accompanied Daisy into the television room and put a film on for her.

He had taken advantage of Samantha last night. Had used her emotions against her—fear of her ex-husband? Her gratitude for Xander's help? The compassion she felt for his past? Take your pick! And then he'd forgotten all of those things in order to take what he wanted.

The fact that Samantha had left his bed before he had woken up, that she was crying this morning, had to mean that she regretted what had happened between the two of them last night.

And Xander had no idea how to put things right between them.

Did he apologise and tell her that he knew and accepted that last night had been a mistake?

Even if it hadn't been?

Did he promise her it would never happen again?

A promise, desiring her as much as he still did, that Xander knew he couldn't keep.

Or did he put her through the even worse embarrassment of being the one to speak first about last night?

No, that last definitely wasn't going to happen; it would totally humiliate Samantha, and that was the last thing Xander ever wanted her to feel in regards to him or their lovemaking.

What he had *wanted* to happen was for the two of them to wake up in each other's arms this morning, to make mind-blowing love again, before they discussed exactly where they were going to go with their relationship.

Except Samantha had already left when he'd woken up this morning.

Consequently there had been no opportunity for a repeat of the night before.

Both of those things telling him that, as far as she was concerned, at least, there was also no relationship for the two of them to discuss.

At the same time as Xander knew they

couldn't continue to live together for the next week without one or both of them saying at least *something* about last night. Acknowledging that it had happened, at least. Not to do so would be juvenile. And their actions last night had been anything but that.

'I'm just going back to the kitchen to have a chat with Mummy, okay, Daisy?' he told the little girl lightly as he raised the volume on the television.

'Okay.' Daisy nodded distractedly, her attention already focused on the animated film on the screen.

Xander closed the door softly behind him as he stepped out into the hallway, drawing in a deep breath once he was outside; he wasn't in the least looking forward to the next few minutes' conversation with Samantha. Or what the outcome of that conversation would mean for the two of them.

Any thoughts of that conversation fled his head the moment he walked back into the kitchen and saw how deathly pale Samantha's face was as she stood as still as a statue, the telephone receiver about to fall from her limp fingers.

'Samantha?' Xander quickly crossed to where she stood to look down searchingly into that pale face as he took that receiver from her and placed it back on the wall, frowning darkly as he saw the pain in those dark amethyst eyes as Samantha stared off into the distance. 'Samantha?'

The way she now looked up at him so blankly, as if she not only didn't see him, but was having trouble even remembering who he was, wasn't in the least reassuring.

Xander lightly clasped the tops of her arms as a way of gaining her attention. 'Samantha!'

'Security just called from Reception downstairs.' She spoke flatly, not an ounce of emotion in her voice as she continued to look up at him blankly.

'And?' he prompted tensely as Samantha didn't add anything to that statement.

She blinked, seeming to come out of her stupor slightly as she finally focused on him. 'Malcolm is downstairs.'

'He is?'

She nodded. 'And apparently he told Security that he has no intention of leaving until he's spoken to one or both of us.'

Xander had known this confrontation was inevitable, had deliberately designed this situation so that Howard would make him the target rather than Samantha and Daisy.

He just hadn't expected it to be this morning, and before he'd even had a chance to talk to Samantha about last night.

CHAPTER TEN

MAYBE IF HE hadn't been so caught up, so blinded by his desire for Samantha and the need he felt to protect her, he would have realised that the bombastic Malcolm Howard was arrogant enough to come to his apartment. Everything Xander had learnt about the other man this past week had indicated he was someone who didn't care about anyone else's feelings, least of all Samantha's.

'I thought you said that your lawyer would contact Malcolm and arrange for him to visit his offices?'

Xander winced at the complete lack of accusation in Samantha's tone. At the lack of any emotion in her voice at all. 'He was going to do that on Monday morning.' He grimaced. 'Obviously I underestimated the speed of Howard's powers of deduction.'

She smiled without humour. 'Don't feel bad about that; a lot of people have underestimated Malcolm's intelligence,' she said flatly.

'I'm so sorry, Samantha.' Xander looked down at her, frowning as he saw her expression was just as unreadable. As if the shock, the possibility of seeing Howard again, had robbed her of all feeling. 'You don't have to do this, Samantha,' he reassured her gently. 'I can go downstairs and tell Howard that my lawyer will contact him on Monday morning as planned.'

Sam knew that would be the safest thing to do. But it was also the coward's thing to do. And she no longer wanted to be that person. 'No,' she said firmly, determinedly rousing herself from the stupor of the shock of knowing that Malcolm was actually downstairs refusing to leave until he had spoken to her. And Xander...

It was her worst nightmare realised.

Well, no, that wasn't strictly true any more; her *worst* nightmare was knowing she had fallen in love with Xander, while understanding that that love wasn't, and never could be, returned.

So, did she want to talk to Malcolm?

Absolutely not.

Did she want this situation between the two of them settled once and for all?

Absolutely yes.

'Is Daisy fully occupied with the TV, do you think?' She chewed worriedly on her bottom lip at thoughts of her young daughter so much as realising that the man who was her father was actually here, in Xander's apartment.

Xander's mouth twisted. 'She's watching one of her favourite animated movies. Very loudly,' he added dryly, as the volume was audible all the way down the hallway.

Sam nodded. 'Then I would rather the two of us talked to Malcolm now, if that's okay with you?' She looked up at Xander expectantly.

'Are you sure?' He frowned darkly, obviously not happy with her decision.

'Just say if *you* aren't comfortable with this.' Sam frowned, noting Xander's pallor, the tightness of his jaw, the nerve pulsing at the base of his throat, and the grimness of his expression. 'You've done so much for us already.'

'The fact that Howard is here at all would seem to imply I didn't do it quickly enough!' He scowled darkly.

'I'm really grateful for all the help you've given me.' Sam frowned as he gave a pained wince. 'I am grateful, Xander, but I can deal with the rest of this on my own if you would rather not be involved any further.'

'That's the last thing I want! Sorry,' he muttered as Samantha flinched at the fierceness of his tone. 'I apologise for raising my voice.'

She grimaced as she placed her hand lightly on Xander's arm. 'Your reaction is perfectly normal, Xander,' she reassured him. 'Believe me, Malcolm has this effect on most people.' She gave his arm a reassuring squeeze before stepping away from him. 'Let's just get this over with, shall we—before I lose my nerve?' she added shakily.

Once this conversation with Malcolm was over, and the matter was hopefully settled, Sam knew then would be the time for her and Xander to talk. If last night had made it awkward for them to continue living together for the next week, this added fiasco with Malcolm could make it impossible!

'I should have been able to protect you from this confrontation,' Xander said.

'Because your instinct is naturally to protect rather than to destroy.'

Xander drew in a sharp breath at the total trust in Samantha's voice. 'We'll talk to Howard in my study,' he stated decisively before picking up the receiver and calling down to Reception, instructing them to send Howard up before ending the call and turning back to Samantha. 'Would you like to go and wait for us in my study, and I'll go and meet Howard at the lift?'

'You really don't have to do this, Xander.'

'Yes, I most certainly do,' he bit out tensely. 'I'm responsible for him being here, and I have absolutely no intention of leaving you to speak with him alone.'

'But—'

'Please go to my study,' he repeated gently

before turning to make his way out into the hallway, deliberately leaving his stick propped against the breakfast bar. The last thing he wanted was to appear physically weak in front of Malcolm Howard.

To that end Xander was leaning casually against the wall outside the lift when the doors opened to reveal his unexpected, and equally unwanted, guest.

His eyes glittered with challenge as Howard stepped out into the corridor. Xander disliked him on sight.

For so many reasons.

For having once mattered to Samantha.

For having been married to her and not appreciating her as the jewel that she was.

For being Daisy's father.

Most of all, for having made both of their lives a misery.

The feeling of dislike was obviously mutual as the older man's face flushed with anger as he looked at Xander. 'Are you aware of the humiliation you caused me last night when I arrived at the club with my date, only to be told

that the almighty Xander Sterne had personally cancelled my membership?'

Xander's top lip curled back with distaste.
Howard believed his ex-wife and daughter were
currently living with Xander in his apartment,
and yet all that was bothering the guy at this
moment was his cancelled membership to one
of his clubs?

Xander's hands clenched into fists at his sides.
Only Samantha's continued faith in him, her
complete belief that he wasn't a violent man
like his father, held him in check.

'You no longer met the criteria of membership
to the Midas nightclub,' he dismissed harshly,
at the same time cursing himself for having
acted so impulsively by cancelling the other
man's membership when he did, prematurely
alerting Howard to his plans.

It had been a stupid reaction on Xander's part,
even petty, and was the reason for Howard's
unwanted presence this morning.

But just the thought of going to Midas one
evening, of seeing this man enjoying himself
in *his* club, a man capable of blackmailing his

ex-wife into going to bed with him, had just been too much for Xander to contemplate. He wasn't sure even Samantha's faith in him would have been enough to prevent him from reacting under those circumstances.

'And what criteria would that be?' the other man challenged. 'No man is allowed to be a member of the Midas nightclub if you are currently sleeping with his ex-wife? If so, then I'm surprised there are any men left in London to fill your club!'

Xander counted to ten in his head. And then counted another ten. And another. And another.

He was determined, he would *not* let Samantha down, and let his temper get the better of him.

'Nothing to say?' Howard challenged.

'I resent even having to breathe the same air as you,' Xander said icily.

Howard's face twisted into an ugly sneer. 'I'm guessing you conveniently forget that aversion when it comes to you sleeping with my ex-wife?'

'Don't say another word,' Xander warned

harshly. 'Not. Another. Word.' A nerve pulsed rapidly in his tightly clenched jaw.

How he would like to knock this man unconscious and put an end to this conversation. Just one little punch to that sneering face, that was all it would take for him to silence Howard and his vile mouth.

But Xander knew he couldn't let himself do it, no matter what the temptation. That he couldn't betray the trust, the belief, that Samantha had in him.

He drew in a deep and controlling breath. 'I have no intention of saying anything else to you without Samantha being present. She's waiting for us in my study.' He didn't wait to see if the other man followed him as he turned and walked down the hallway, ignoring the jarring pain in his leg as he did so.

Welcoming that pain if it stopped him from giving in to the anger now consuming him.

Malcolm Howard was supposed to have loved Samantha and Daisy, protected them both, and instead he'd deliberately hurt them.

How could Samantha have ever thought

she was in love with such a man, let alone married him?

But Xander knew exactly how. From their conversations he knew she had been very young and completely alone in the world when she and Howard had met.

No doubt she had been flattered by the attentions of this older and seemingly charming and sophisticated man. The man she had trusted to love and take care of her.

Xander turned to look at the other man coldly as he paused outside the closed door to his study. 'Know this, Howard—if you hurt Samantha again, then I would also advise that you keep a watchful eye over your shoulder in the future.' He showed his teeth in a feral smile.

Howard's face flushed angrily. 'Are you threatening me?'

'That wasn't a threat, it was a promise,' Xander assured him softly as he opened the study door before standing back to allow Howard to enter the room ahead of him.

Xander followed close behind him and saw that Samantha was standing by the window,

the sun shining into the room behind her pre-
venting him—and consequently Howard, too—
from being able to make out her expression. But
Xander could tell by the stiffness of her slender
shoulders, and the way her hands were clasped
tightly together in front of her, that the next few
minutes were going to be an ordeal for her.

He crossed the room to stand in front of her,
deliberately blocking her from Howard's view,
as he took both of her icy-cold hands in his.
He was able to see how white her face was
now, casting those freckles across her nose and
cheeks into sharp relief, and her eyes were dark
with unspoken pain as she looked up at him
trustingly.

Xander vowed there and then that he would
never, could never, let down or betray this warm
and vulnerable woman's trust in him.

'Ready?' he asked softly.

Sam wasn't sure she would ever be ready for
what she knew was going to be a very unpleasant confrontation with her ex-husband. And she
still felt guilty, as well as grateful, that Xander
had become so deeply involved in her personal

problems. Admittedly, he had asked to be involved, but she doubted that when he had he'd realised just how unpleasant this situation was going to get. She had known from his expression earlier that he certainly hadn't imagined her ex-husband would turn up at his apartment this morning.

'Touching as this scene undoubtedly is,' Malcolm bit out scornfully behind them, 'perhaps you could take your hands off my ex-wife long enough for the three of us to actually *have* this conversation!'

Sam had taken advantage of Xander's short absence to steel herself against showing any reaction to seeing Malcolm again, but there was no way she could stop the nausea that now roiled in her stomach as she listened to his sarcastic taunt. She should have remembered that words had always been Malcolm's weapon of choice.

'Ignore him and look at me,' Xander urged softly, his hands tightening about hers as she did as he asked and looked up into his warm and compassionate eyes. 'Whatever happens, know that I'm here to protect you and Daisy,' he encouraged gruffly. 'That I won't let him hurt either of you.'

Grateful tears now blurred Sam's vision even as she straightened her spine determinedly. 'Let's do this.' She nodded.

'Well done,' Xander murmured, giving her hands a last squeeze before releasing them. 'When I move away, go and sit behind the desk,' he told her softly. 'It will give you a degree of power,' he explained as she eyed him quizzically.

Sam smiled, sure that Xander had used that degree of power a few times himself. 'Thank you,' she mouthed before stepping to the side and then past him, noting Malcolm sprawled comfortably in the chair on the opposite side of the desk even as she seated herself in the high-back leather chair behind it.

She was aware of Xander moving to stand with his back leaning against the wall behind her so he could look directly at Malcolm.

Her gaze was icy as she looked across the

desk at her ex-husband. 'This conversation should have been left to our lawyers.'

Malcolm's top lip curled back in a sneer. 'My, my, how brave you've become since you began sharing the bed of a billionaire.'

'Stop this right now, Malcolm.' Sam glared across the width of the desk at him as she heard Xander pushing fiercely away from the wall behind her.

'So defensive on your lover's behalf,' Malcolm continued as he eyed the younger man speculatively. 'Nothing to say for yourself, Sterne?' His voice hardened challengingly.

Xander had hoped, with the help of his warning out in the hallway, that this conversation might have at least given a semblance of civility. The older man's continued and insulting aggression told him that wasn't going to happen.

'I don't feel the need to defend myself to men like you,' Xander scorned. 'Weak men, who take pleasure in hurting women and children.'

The older man snorted. 'I don't remember hearing Sam complaining at the time.'

'Maybe you just weren't listening?'

Howard's expression darkened. 'You—'

'Let's just get to the point of this meeting, shall we?' Xander sighed wearily, not sure how much longer he was willing to put up with this man's insulting behaviour.

'I haven't finished.'

'Oh, you're finished,' Xander assured the other man coldly. 'You just aren't smart enough to know when you're down, let alone out!'

Howard's face twisted into fury as he sat forward tensely. 'You arrogant bast—'

'Not quite, I believe my parents had been married for almost seven months when my twin and I were born,' Xander interrupted dismissively.

'I meant figuratively not literally.'

'Okay, I'll start this conversation, if you won't.' Xander stared at the other man coldly. 'For the past week you have been experiencing difficulties, in obtaining a business loan from a certain bank, I believe.'

The older man surged angrily to his feet. 'Are you saying you're responsible for that too?'

Xander gave Samantha a rueful glance. 'I thought you said he was intelligent?'

She shrugged. 'I believed he was.'

'Obviously you were wrong.' Xander smiled. 'So, let's just cut to the chase, shall we, Howard? My lawyer has already drawn up a contract, which you *will* go to his office and sign on Monday morning, which declares that you agree to give Samantha the divorce settlement of one million pounds that you should have given her three years ago, as well as giving up all and any claim to Daisy, with the added agreement that you will make no attempt to see either one of them ever again.'

'Are you completely insane?' Howard laughed incredulously.

It was everything Sam wanted, of course—except the million pounds. She didn't want anything for herself, least of all Malcolm's money. All she wanted was the freedom to know that she need never again fear Malcolm making any sort of claim on Daisy.

But she wasn't stupid enough to turn the money down either if it was given, knew that with a million pounds she would be able to put most of the money into trust for Daisy, and that the rest would allow her to raise her daughter without worrying where every penny came from.

Was Xander really capable of intimidating Malcolm into agreeing to sign such a one-sided contract? One look at the cold determination in his face was enough to answer that.

'I really should listen to Xander if I were you, Malcolm.'

'Do you think I give a damn about the opinion of a little nonentity like *you*?' Malcolm turned on Sam sneeringly. 'You might be feeling all brave and fearless right now, but let's just wait and see how brave you're feeling once Sterne gets bored with you and kicks you out of his bed.' Malcolm seemed to flinch then as Xander stepped forward threateningly.

Control it, Xander told himself as he came to a halt just inches away from the other man. *Keep it together. Don't do this. Don't let this man bait you into doing something you'll regret.*

Especially don't lose it in front of Samantha.

That would surely be unforgivable when she continued to look at him so trustingly.

His eyes glittered down at the other man in warning. 'Maybe you should consider putting some respect in your tone when you talk to Samantha?'

The older man gave a snort. 'Why should it matter to you how I talk to her?'

'All you need to know is that it does,' Xander stated coldly.

'And maybe *you* should stop giving her the false hope that you actually care?' Howard scoffed. 'Okay, so you're enjoying playing the part of the White Knight right now, but we both know she's just an amusement to you, a pretty toy to warm your bed for a while. But only until you get bored with her and move on to the next conquest.'

The scornful taunt was so close to what Sam already knew was going to happen between herself and Xander, and sooner rather than later, that she couldn't help but feel the pain of it twisting deep inside her.

Which was exactly the reaction Malcolm had hoped for.

She was made of stronger stuff than that. Was bigger than Malcolm. Was certainly a far better person than he could ever be.

And so was Xander.

'Xander,' Sam cut in determinedly, 'you do realise that if you give in to the impulse you feel to hit him, that you'll have to disinfect your hand afterwards?' Somehow Sam managed to keep her voice light and mocking as she remained seated behind the desk—the latter because she doubted her legs would support her if she attempted to stand!

It was possible to visibly see the tension leave Xander's shoulders as she taunted Malcolm, those dark brown eyes glowing with admiration, an approving smile slowly curving those sculpted lips.

Sam shakily returned that smile, dearly hoping she looked more confident than she felt.

Xander's warmth faded as he turned back to face the other man. 'Which of us is the more powerful, do you think, Howard?' he mused dryly. 'How long do you think you'll be able to continue to be in business if I don't come through with that loan? And how long would you continue to be invited to the fashionable parties you so enjoy, if I should decide to make my aversion to you public? How many restaurants would suddenly find they have no tables available? How many of London's elite would begin to question *why* it is I find you so obnoxious?'

'Because you're obviously having an affair with my ex-wife!' the other man blustered.

'I work for him,' Sam corrected firmly, decisively, her gaze hardening as she realised from Malcolm's bluster just how weak he really was. 'You *will* go to Xander's lawyer, Malcolm. You will sign the contract. And then you will never show your face anywhere that I might ever see it again. Because if you don't,' she continued coldly as Malcolm would have spoken, 'I will let Xander ruin you.'

Xander had never admired Samantha more than he did at that moment. She looked magnificent. All fiery eyed, and with her hair like a living flame about her shoulders.

Howard breathed hard. 'And if I do sign this contract what guarantee do I have that you'll keep your side of the bargain?'

'You have my own and Samantha's word on it,' Xander answered the other man harshly. 'And, unlike you, Samantha's integrity is un-impeachable. My own word, again unlike your own, is completely dependable as well as deeply respected.'

The older man's face twisted into an ugly mask. 'Why the hell should I give you that power?'

'Because I *will* take delight in ruining you if you don't sign the contract?' Xander retorted mildly.

Howard snorted. 'I would be living with the sword of Damocles hanging over my head for the rest of my life!'

'Better than having it thrust into your cold dead heart,' Xander countered unsympatheti-cally.

Howard eyed him for several long moments,

obviously fighting an inner battle with himself; arrogance as opposed to good sense. 'Okay, I'll sign your blasted contract!' he finally burst out fiercely as the latter obviously won. 'But you had better make sure you keep to your side of the bargain.'

'I just said I would,' Xander rasped, wishing this man would just go now. He so badly needed to hold Samantha, to comfort her, to take away that lost look he could see in her eyes.

Malcolm eyed them both scornfully. 'The two of you are welcome to each other.'

'Is that really the best you can do?' Sam asked, wondering why she had ever been frightened of this man. Certainly wondering how she could ever have thought she was in love with him!

'Oh, and, Malcolm,' she added as he turned to where Xander now pointedly held the door open for him to leave, waiting until she had Malcolm's full attention before continuing, 'for the record, you were too damned selfish to ever know what I liked in bed!'

His face darkened as he took a threatening step back towards her.

'I ought to just—'

A little red-haired whirlwind dashed past an obviously surprised Xander to enter the study and begin kicking Malcolm's shins. 'Don't you dare hurt my mummy!'

Malcolm looked stunned for several seconds and then he reached down to grasp his daughter's shoulders in an attempt to hold her away from him. 'It's Daddy, Daisy.'

'You're not my daddy! Daddies are nice, and you're mean,' Daisy stormed. 'I hate you!' Tears streamed down Daisy's face as she continued to kick him.

Sam had been so stunned when Daisy rushed so unexpectedly into the room that for a few seconds she had been completely unable to react. But she now rose quickly to her feet before rushing round the desk to pull Daisy away from Malcolm and take her into her arms. 'It's all right, darling,' she assured Daisy as hot tears coursed down both their cheeks. She held her daughter tightly in her arms. 'Everything is going to be all right. I promise.'

Daisy clung to her. 'Make him go away, Xander! Make him go away!' She sobbed into Sam's shoulder.

Sam looked appealingly at a white-faced Xander over the top of Daisy's head, giving a choked sob as she watched him grasp hold of the back of Malcolm's shirt before pulling the other man out of the room and closing the door behind them.

Leaving Sam the privacy she needed to calm and soothe her broken-hearted daughter.

'Whew, it's been quite a day.' Xander sat in an armchair in the sitting room later that evening, Samantha seated opposite. And if Xander felt emotionally exhausted by the events of the day, then Samantha still looked shell-shocked.

'Daisy and I have to leave.'

'What?' Xander sat forward, frowning darkly at Samantha's quietly spoken comment.

Sam focused on him with effort; she was so tired she just wanted to crawl into bed, pull the covers over her head, and stay there for the rest of the weekend.

It was not going to happen, of course.

Once Sam had calmed Daisy down, promising her daughter over and over again that she would never see that horrible man again, Daisy had seemed to recover, with the resilience of all small children, from her emotional outburst. Xander's suggestion, when he returned to the study a few minutes later, of them all going to the cinema to see the film that Daisy wanted to see had clinched the deal.

Whereas Sam's recovery had all been a front, for Daisy's sake, and later that day she had found the tears slipping silently down her face as she stared up unseeingly at the animated film on the big screen in front of her. The feel of Xander's comforting fingers curling about hers in the darkness had been her complete undoing, and she had found herself falling slowly towards him, her head resting on his shoulder as she continued to quietly sob.

The rest of the day had been a blur, something to be endured rather than enjoyed. Xander had taken them all for a pizza after the cinema, and then read Daisy a story and tucked her up in bed after Sam had given her daughter her evening bath.

Upsetting as Daisy's outburst to Malcolm had been, it was Xander who was now at the centre of Sam's concerns.

Sam had realised today that it wasn't just Daisy who had come to rely on him too much this past week. She was also guilty of leaning on him. Depending on him too much.

And it had to stop.

Oh, she wouldn't dream of stopping Xander from continuing to see Daisy, if he wanted to; that would just be too cruel when her daughter so obviously adored him.

But Sam's own dependence on him had to end.

Right now.

'I think, after all that's happened, that Daisy and I have to leave. I can't tell you how grateful I am for all you've done for Daisy and me, but—'

'I don't want your gratitude, Samantha!'

'Nevertheless, you have it,' Sam insisted quietly, eyes downcast so that she didn't have to look at him. So she didn't have to acknowledge how much she loved him. 'You're recovering more and more every day, and I'm pretty sure you can manage on your own now. Malcolm is too scared now, of what he knows you can do to him, to ever bother us again. You're more than welcome to continue seeing Daisy, of course.'

'How generous of you!'

Sam winced at the sarcasm in Xander's voice. 'Please don't be angry, Xander.'

'What the hell do you expect me to be?' He ran an agitated hand through the blond thickness of his hair as he surged to his feet. 'What about last night, Samantha?' He frowned darkly. 'What about *us*?'

She gave a sad shake of her head. 'There is no us. There never could be.'

'You don't know that.'

'Yes, I do!' she said vehemently. 'Last night was— Well, it was wonderful,' she acknowledged huskily. 'But it can't happen again. And my staying on here, under those circumstances, would just be—I need to leave, Xander, can't you see that?' She looked up at him imploringly, silently pleading with him not to make this any harder for her than it already was.

The last thing she wanted was to leave him. How could it not be, when she was in love with him?

But they had come together under far from perfect circumstances. And Xander had been wonderful, amazing, both with Daisy, and with helping Sam deal with Malcolm once and for all. But Sam wasn't about to take advantage of his generous nature by allowing him to feel even more responsibility towards her because of what had happened between the two of them last night.

'I need to leave,' she repeated as she stood up with determination. 'Please don't make this any harder for me than it already is,' she added firmly as she could see Xander was about to make another protest. 'Daisy and I will be leaving in the morning. But I would appreciate it if you were able to see Daisy again. She loves you so much,' she added gruffly, knowing that she loved Xander as much as, if not more than, her daughter did. Just as she knew it was breaking her heart to leave him.

Xander had never felt so impotent in his life as he did at this moment, knowing by the expression on Samantha's face that she meant what she said. That she had also made it clear that last night hadn't meant the same to her as it had to him. That she really did intend leaving him tomorrow.

And there wasn't a thing he could do or say to stop her.

CHAPTER ELEVEN

One month later.

'WHEN ARE YOU going to stop brooding and go and claim your woman?'

Xander hadn't heard his brother open the door as he leant back in his chair staring sightlessly—broodingly—out of the window of his office at the Midas Enterprises building in London.

He turned now to glare at Darius as his brother leant casually against the doorframe. 'I'm far too busy to deal with your warped sense of humour today, Darius!' he snarled aggressively as he straightened in his chair.

Darius straightened slowly before crossing the room. 'I can see that.' A mocking smile curved his lips as he looked down at Xander's obviously empty desk. 'I thought you might like to know I've just come back from visiting Miranda at the dance studio.'

Xander tensed. 'And why should that interest me?'

Topaz eyes gleamed with amusement. "Possibly because I saw Sam too while I was there?'

Xander felt a painful lurch in his chest; he hadn't spoken privately to Samantha for four and a half weeks. Not since the day they had routed Howard so completely, and afterwards she'd told him she was leaving him the following morning. She'd then packed her bags and done exactly that.

He had tried to talk her out of it, of course. But Samantha had been stubbornly determined. She had again thanked him very politely for all his help, and reassured him he really was well enough to take care of himself now. That he didn't need her any more.

That he didn't *need* her any more?

Xander wasn't even sure he had drawn in breath without pain since Samantha left him that Sunday morning. He knew that not a moment went by when he didn't think about her. When he didn't want to see her, to just be with her again.

And he had been absolutely correct about his apartment having all the warmth of a morgue, once Samantha and Daisy were no longer living there with him. He now avoided being there as much as possible.

Xander's mouth tightened. 'Samantha has made her lack of interest in seeing me again very obvious, Darius.' *More* than obvious.

'Strange, she always asks how you are whenever I see her at Miranda's studio,' his brother told him softly.

Xander stood up abruptly to cross the room and stand in front of the floor-to-ceiling windows, his back to the room as he looked out blindly. 'She's just being polite, because she's grateful that I helped rid her of Howard from her life once and for all.'

Howard had duly kept his appointment at the lawyer's office, and neither Xander nor Samantha had needed to be present when the other man signed the contract. Howard had also paid Samantha's belated divorce settlement, and she and Daisy were now renting a two-bedroom apartment overlooking a park. Samantha had still taken up the part-time job at Andy's dance studio, and the two women had become even firmer friends, according to his sister-in-law.

Darius joined Xander by the window. 'Sam doesn't look well today, Xander.'

He turned sharply to look at his brother. 'What do you mean? What's wrong with her?' he demanded, frowning darkly.

'How would I know?' Darius shrugged.

Xander's scowl deepened. 'Maybe because your wife is Samantha's best friend as well as her employer?'

Darius eyed him pityingly. 'And Miranda and I have far better things to do than talk about Sam when we're alone together.'

'You are so annoying.' Xander turned abruptly to stride determinedly across his office and collect his coat from the back of his chair before quickly pulling it on.

'Where are you going?'

He shot his twin an angry glare as he strode over to the door. 'Out!' He ignored Darius's chuckle as he wrenched the door open before striding impatiently out into the hallway towards the lift.

He wasn't in the least surprised to find the car, and driver, waiting for him downstairs as he stepped outside the building; Darius might be annoying, but he could read his twin like a book.

'I'll drive myself, thank you, Paul.' He managed to smile at the other man as he took the keys from him to get in behind the wheel.

Xander felt more light-hearted than he had for the past four weeks as he drove through the busy London streets towards Andy's dance studio. He knew it was because he was going to see Samantha again. Was going to talk to her again.

Whether or not Samantha would be as pleased to see him was another matter.

'Dare I hope that you're finally here to see Sam?' his sister-in-law teased as he entered her dance studio a short time later, obviously having just finished taking her last dance class of the day.

Xander narrowed his eyes. 'You and Darius should seriously think about becoming a comedy team.'

Andy gave a husky laugh. 'Sam's in the office. If you're interested, that is?'

'Oh, I'm interested,' Xander confirmed determinedly.

'Good luck!'

Xander had no doubt he was going to need it!

'Samantha?'

Sam stilled as she heard the husky sound of Xander's voice in her head.

A voice she had heard so many times, and in exactly the same husky tone, these past few weeks. When she was here at work. Or at home with Daisy in their new apartment. When she lay alone in her bed at night.

And each time she heard it Sam felt a twisting pain in her chest. As evidence of the empty hollowness inside her, that she knew only Xander could fill. But never would.

She closed her lids as her eyes suddenly filled with scalding tears, silently willing them not to fall. Wishing the pain of loving Xander would stop. But knowing it never would.

'Samantha?'

Sam almost jumped out of her chair, her heart pounded erratically in her chest, as she felt caressing fingers against her cheek, her eyes widening with disbelief as she found herself looking up at Xander.

He was the suave and sophisticated Xander Sterne today, successful billionaire business-man. A man so unlike the casually dressed Xander she had known and grown to love four weeks ago. Today he wore a dark, sleekly tai-lored suit and shirt, with a meticulously knot-ted tie, and his hair was professionally styled rather than the overlong and shaggy look he had favoured a month ago.

But it was the changes in his face that now caused Sam to frown; his cheeks seemed thin-ner even than the weekend, the last time he had called and picked Daisy up for the day, with deep grooves beside his mouth and eyes, and his mouth was a grim and uncompromis-ing line.

Her throat moved convulsively as she swallowed, still not completely sure he was really here or just a figment of her aching imagination. 'Are you real?'

He gave a rueful smile. 'Unfortunately for you, yes, I'm very much real.'

Sam's frown deepened. 'Unfortunately for me?' She had never been so pleased to see anyone in her life before as she was Xander.

Just to be alone in the same room with him. To be able to drink him in: how he looked, how he moved, how he *smelled*.

'That last evening at my apartment you made it pretty clear that you had no interest in seeing me again.'

'I did?' The whole of that last day in his apartment had become something of a hazy dream to Sam the past few weeks.

'You did,' Xander confirmed grimly as he stepped away from her before thrusting his hands into his trousers pockets. 'Are you okay, Samantha?' He could see what Darius meant now; without Daisy as her protective shield, Samantha's cheeks were pale and hollow, those beautiful amethyst-coloured eyes dark and haunted.

'Has Howard been bothering you again?'

'No, absolutely not,' she assured him hastily. 'I'm pretty sure we've all seen and heard the last of him. And Daisy loves our new apartment. She so much enjoys going to the park after school.'

'I'm so glad to hear that. But I asked how *you* were, Samantha,' he said gruffly.

Her gaze now avoided meeting his. 'I love working here at the studio with Andy, and to no longer have any money worries—'

'That isn't what I was asking, either. Sorry,' Xander apologised as he realised he had raised his voice. 'I didn't mean to shout.' He grimaced. 'I just—I've missed you, Samantha.'

'You have?' she gasped softly.

Xander nodded abruptly. 'Very much. I— Look, will you have dinner with me this evening?' A nerve pulsed in his jaw as he waited for her answer.

Sam stared up at him, not altogether sure she had heard him correctly. Why would Xander invite her out to dinner with him? 'I really am okay, Xander,' she assured him ruefully. 'Malcolm signed the contract, and paid the divorce settlement into my account. I'm happy working here, and nicely settled into the new apartment. Daisy is happy—'

'I don't give a—!' Xander broke off, breathing heavily as he ran one agitated hand through the heavy thickness of his blond hair. 'Well. Yes.' He grimaced. 'Of course I care about those things, Samantha. But I'm asking you out to dinner for *me,* not so that we talk about your new flat, or how much Daisy loves the park or how she's doing at school.'

She gave a puzzled shake of her head. 'I don't understand.'

'Obviously not,' he muttered. 'Samantha, I'm trying to ask you out on a date, and all you keep doing is talking about everything else. Do you have any idea how frustrating that is? How irritating it is to have you keep telling me how good your life is now, when my own is completely messed up?'

'It is?'

He nodded abruptly. 'I can't eat or sleep. I can't *think*.'

Sam could barely breathe as a faint glimmer of hope began to burn in her chest. A hint of light in the heaviness that had been weighing her down for so many weeks. 'Why not?'

He gave a groan. 'Why do you think?'

She gave a cautious shake of her head. 'I have no idea.'

'Because I'm in love with you, damn it!' His eyes gleamed darkly. 'I'm so in love with you that nothing and no else is important to me any more. Not my family. Not my business. Just you. I can't think of anything else *but* you. Of how much I miss you. How much I want you and Daisy back in my life. How much I love you.'

'But you let me go,' Sam breathed softly.

'Because you said you *wanted* to go!'

'That was because—' Sam drew in a deep and steadying breath, totally stunned at having Xander tell her he loved her. Xander *loved* her? 'I didn't want to leave, Xander. I just thought— You had been so good to me already, saving me from Malcolm, being so patient and caring with Daisy. I didn't want you to let me stay because you felt sorry for me, or because you were still trying to protect me. I couldn't bear that.' Her voice broke emotionally. 'If you couldn't think of me as your equal—'

'I don't think of you as being my equal, Samantha. I think of you as being so much better than I could ever be—and I *adore* you for it!' He began to pace the room. 'But I didn't want you to stay with me out of gratitude, either. Just because I had helped you sort out the situation with Howard.'

'I don't,' Samantha assured him. 'Well, of course I'm grateful...' she smiled ruefully '... but that's certainly not the reason I—that I made love with you the night before that awful confrontation with Malcolm.'

'It isn't?'

'Absolutely not.'

There was no way that Xander could doubt Samantha's sincerity. 'Then why did you?' He gave an impatient shake of his head. 'Do you have any idea how much I've missed you?

How empty my apartment is without you in it? How empty my bed is without you in it?' He breathed raggedly. 'I'm going quietly insane here, Samantha; so please will you say *something*?'

Sam stood up slowly, that glimmer of light bursting into full brilliance inside her as the heavy weight of unhappiness evaporated and left as if it had never been. 'I didn't want to leave you, Xander. I thought you just felt sorry for me, and I didn't want that from you. You had done so much for me already, I thought the least I could do was leave you in peace.'

'Peace? I've been in living hell without you!' he insisted fiercely.

She reached up to gently touch the side of his face. 'Xander, the only reason I left that day was because I realised I'd fallen in love with you, and I didn't want you to feel in the least pressured to—to continue the relationship because you felt sorry for me.'

'What?'

She smiled shakily. 'I'm in love with you, Xander. So much that it *hurts*. You asked how

I've been? Well, I've been just awful. I can't eat. I can't sleep. I think about you all the time. I *miss* you all the time.'

'Can we both really have been that stupid?' Xander gazed down at her in wonder.

Sam gave a tremulous smile. 'It certainly looks like it.'

His expression softened as he took her into his arms in a crushing hold. 'I love you!' he groaned achingly into her hair. 'I love you, Samantha. Do you have any idea what it meant to me—how much I value that you believed in me, trusted me, when I didn't?'

'And look how right I was about that,' she said huskily. 'Your protectiveness of those weaker than yourself is a blessing, Xander, and has absolutely nothing to do with men like your father and my ex-husband.'

Xander's arms tightened. 'I've felt so empty without you in my life, Samantha.'

'Me too, without you.' Sam held onto him just as tightly.

'Does that mean you'll marry me?'

Sam opened startled eyes. 'Marry you?'

Xander's hands moved up to cradle each side of her face as he looked down with all of his love for her shining in his eyes. 'You don't have to marry me immediately if it's too soon for you. Just tell me that you'll be my wife one day very soon.' His hands trembled. 'I love you so very much, my darling Samantha, and I can't bear the thought of not being with you for ever now that I know you love me too.'

It was more, so much more than Sam had ever thought, had ever imagined might happen in her life.

Xander loved her.

As she loved him.

And she couldn't bear the thought of the two of them not being together for ever either.

'Yes, I'll marry you, Xander,' she answered him exultantly.

'You will?' He looked down at her wonderingly.

'I will.'

'When?'

'Next week? Tomorrow?' She laughed huskily as she saw the urgency in Xander's expression.

He grinned. 'I want you to have a big white wedding. In a church. Surrounded by all our friends and family. Daisy can be your bridesmaid.'

Sam was sure it wasn't accidental that Xander was describing a wedding that was the exact opposite of that hurried union to Malcolm in a register office six years ago. Or that Daisy would be a large part of that ceremony.

Xander was tacitly telling her their marriage, his love for her and Daisy, would be nothing like her previous one.

As if Sam had ever thought otherwise.

She hadn't thought it possible, but she loved Xander more than ever at that moment, and she knew she always would.

'It sounds perfect.' She beamed up at him.

'*You're* perfect,' he assured her warmly. 'I promise you we'll be so happy together, Samantha. We can buy a house, with a garden for Daisy, and—'

'And have more children?' Sam ventured cautiously. 'I always wanted a big family,' she explained shyly.

'Then we'll have a houseful of children,' Xander promised her. 'As long as I have you to love, and you to love me, then I'll be happy.'

It was all that Sam could ever have hoped or wished for...and more.

EPILOGUE

'WHAT ARE WE looking at, Daddy?' Daisy asked in a loud whisper.

'I'm not too sure,' Xander muttered, Daisy sitting on his knee as the two of them frowned at the monitor in front of them, his free hand tightly holding onto Samantha's as she lay on the bed beside them.

'It doesn't look much like a baby, Daddy,' Daisy said doubtfully as they watched the movements being projected from inside Samantha's womb onto the monitor.

Xander felt his panic rise; it didn't look like any baby he had ever seen either. Admittedly there was the thud-thud sound of a heartbeat, but even that sounded too rapid, and there were definitely too many legs visible—

'That's because it's two babies, darling,' Samantha murmured indulgently.

'What?' Xander gasped.

'Two babies,' she repeated emotionally.

'Two babies,' Xander echoed faintly, realising that must be the reason the heartbeat sounded too rapid: because it was two heartbeats, not one.

'It would seem that we're having twins, darling,' Samantha assured him lovingly.

He swallowed, his mouth dry. 'I can't— We can't—'

'Of course we can.' She smiled indulgently. 'You're a twin,' she reminded him calmly.

'Twins.' Xander put Daisy down to stand up and hug his wife. 'We're having twins!' he cried, tears of happiness shining in his eyes.

'Yes, we are.' Samantha laughed huskily as she hugged him back.

He gave a sudden groan as he slowly released her before straightening. 'You do realise Darius is never going to stop teasing me?' he explained as Samantha gave him a questioning glance.

'He won't,' she assured him.

'Of course he will.' Xander groaned again.

'He really won't.' Sam laughed softly, her

heart bursting with love for the man who had been her husband for this past wonderful year. 'Andy told me yesterday that the two of them are expecting twins too!'

'Hah!' Xander gave a grin of triumph. 'My mother and Charles are going to be thrilled at the idea of more grandchildren!'

Sam couldn't have asked for nicer in-laws than Catherine and Charles, and they absolutely adored Daisy. She had no doubt there was plenty of room in those two kind hearts for a dozen more grandchildren.

'Wait.' Xander gave a teasing grimace. 'How will I cope if it's two girls and I have three little Samanthas twisting me round their little fingers?' He gazed down at Daisy, whom he absolutely adored and who adored him back.

'Look on the bright side, darling,' Sam teased. 'It could be two little Xanders to twist me round their little fingers!'

'Would you like to know the sex of your two babies?' the technician asked softly.

Sam looked at Xander and Xander looked at

Sam, and then both of them shook their heads at the same time.

Sons, or more daughters, they would love all of their children.

As much as they loved and adored each other.

* * * * *

MILLS & BOON®
Large Print – July 2015

THE TAMING OF XANDER STERNE
Carole Mortimer

IN THE BRAZILIAN'S DEBT
Susan Stephens

AT THE COUNT'S BIDDING
Caitlin Crews

THE SHEIKH'S SINFUL SEDUCTION
Dani Collins

THE REAL ROMERO
Cathy Williams

HIS DEFIANT DESERT QUEEN
Jane Porter

PRINCE NADIR'S SECRET HEIR
Michelle Conder

THE RENEGADE BILLIONAIRE
Rebecca Winters

THE PLAYBOY OF ROME
Jennifer Faye

REUNITED WITH HER ITALIAN EX
Lucy Gordon

HER KNIGHT IN THE OUTBACK
Nikki Logan

MILLS & BOON®
Large Print – August 2015

THE BILLIONAIRE'S BRIDAL BARGAIN
Lynne Graham

AT THE BRAZILIAN'S COMMAND
Susan Stephens

CARRYING THE GREEK'S HEIR
Sharon Kendrick

THE SHEIKH'S PRINCESS BRIDE
Annie West

HIS DIAMOND OF CONVENIENCE
Maisey Yates

OLIVERO'S OUTRAGEOUS PROPOSAL
Kate Walker

THE ITALIAN'S DEAL FOR I DO
Jennifer Hayward

THE MILLIONAIRE AND THE MAID
Michelle Douglas

EXPECTING THE EARL'S BABY
Jessica Gilmore

BEST MAN FOR THE BRIDESMAID
Jennifer Faye

IT STARTED AT A WEDDING...
Kate Hardy

0715 Rom LP

MILLS & BOON®

Why shop at millsandboon.co.uk?

Each year, thousands of romance readers find their perfect read at millsandboon.co.uk. That's because we're passionate about bringing you the very best romantic fiction. Here are some of the advantages of shopping at www.millsandboon.co.uk:

* **Get new books first**—you'll be able to buy your favourite books one month before they hit the shops

* **Get exclusive discounts**—you'll also be able to buy our specially created monthly collections, with up to 50% off the RRP

* **Find your favourite authors**—latest news, interviews and new releases for all your favourite authors and series on our website, plus ideas for what to try next

* **Join in**—once you've bought your favourite books, don't forget to register with us to rate, review and join in the discussions

Visit **www.millsandboon.co.uk**
for all this and more today!